Totally Bound Publishing books by Sara Ohlin

Graciella
Handling the Rancher
Seducing the Dragonfly

Rescue Me
Salvaging Love

Graciella

SEDUCING THE DRAGONFLY

SARA OHLIN

Seducing the Dragonfly
ISBN # 978-1-83943-865-3
©Copyright Sara Ohlin 2020
Cover Art by Erin Dameron-Hill ©Copyright March 2020
Interior text design by Claire Siemaszkiewicz
Totally Bound Publishing

SEDUCING THE DRAGONFLY

Dedication

For Megan, the best sister anyone could have. I appreciate your support more than you could ever know. Let's meet in Paris again someday!
Je t'aime!

Chapter One

"We have five acquisitions in the works, including the two connecting properties in Bergmannkeiz. Those are going to be an albatross around our necks, or, preferably, like spinning thread into gold. Things are changing rapidly. We need to stay ahead of our competition and the trends. That's why we're successful. But we won't be if we keep slacking off. Gabe, make sure you're ready for our Frankfurt trip. Focus your research on demographic shifts and traffic patterns. I shouldn't have to tell you how to do your job." Turner barely looked at his staff as he gave them orders.

Nine a.m. and it feels like midnight. Routine Monday morning meeting and he could barely think straight. His agenda blurred in front of him.

"I need the financial analysis on the five acquisitions finished and on my desk at the end of the day. Rebecca, you're on Bergmannkeiz. I don't want your thoughts on the long-term profit strategy. I need data."

"The end of the day, sir? The entire analysis?"

Turner shot his eyes toward his best financial planner. "This is the second extension I've given you." His temper shot like sparks through an electrical wire, angry, uncontrollable. Shit, he was tired. "Miss Graves, more coffee. Please," he yelled through the open door of his office. Not sleeping for several weeks was dragging him through the mud. Fucking nightmares of Brockman Farms. His own fucking albatross.

"Right, Mr. Brockman. You do remember we've been waiting for the tax assessment?" He *did* know that. Meeting Miss Graves halfway across the room, he took the mug she offered and faced the city.

From his wall of windows on the twenty-sixth floor of the Sony Center Office Tower in Berlin, Turner could see the red brick Kollhoff Tower and the city beyond. New Berlin, they called it, much of Potsdamer Platz having been rebuilt after the fall of the Berlin Wall. It was a modern city dominated by steel and glass, boasting four-star restaurants, world-class shopping, glitzy hotels and apartments.

With his keen sense of planning, design and eye for location, Turner had worked with the top architects and business developers to polish Berlin's shiny new look. This job provided him with an office at the top, more money than he knew what to do with and a sense of power.

Power. Something he'd been searching for his entire life. Something he'd never had at the farm.

No matter how far he got, how hard he tried, he could never purge the small town of Graciella, Oregon, from his mind. He'd been all over the world searching for control, and he'd found it, commanded it, buried his memories in it, because he'd been powerless in the one place it mattered, against his father. Now he felt the frayed edges of his conscience coming undone. For

Christ's sake, he was yelling at his team. And his team was amazing. They could do his job for him.

Turner had no intention of ever seeing Brockman Farms again, even now, with his father dead and buried months ago. Unfortunately, he'd been plagued by insomnia, a bastard of a headache and memories of Graciella every night for the past three weeks. Memories he would have sworn he'd annihilated.

"Mr. Brockman—"

"What?" he snapped at his secretary before he could rein in his emotions. He rubbed his temples and forced a calmness he didn't feel into his tone. "I'm sorry, Miss Graves, what did you need?"

"Mr. Klein would like to see you in his office. Now, sir."

"Right." He followed her out and strode down the hall to the office of Hans Klein, his boss and CEO of Klein Development Strategies.

"Ah, Turner. Have a seat," Hans said. An imposing man in his late fifties, at six feet tall, two hundred pounds and with silver hair, it was the sly gleam in his eyes that had people snapping to attention in his presence. Hans was known internationally for being one of the top business developers, shrewd and cunning with his eye on absolute success and profit. Turner was one of the few who knew there was a softer side to the man, that he enjoyed playing with his grandchildren more than designing stunning office towers, for instance. In turn, Hans was one of a handful of people Turner trusted.

"How's Melanie?" Turner asked.

Hans' smile warmed. "Lovely as ever. We're going sailing this weekend. She asked if you'd join us. I told her you wouldn't be available."

"I'd love to…what? We don't start work on the new residential development until Monday. Do you need me in Frankfurt early?"

Hans sat on the edge of his desk, facing Turner. "You're not going to Frankfurt. You're going home to Oregon."

Uncrossing his legs and standing gave Turner the few seconds he needed to maintain a sense of calm. But he barely controlled the anger and confusion in the glare he tossed at Hans.

"Oh, don't pull that warrior bullshit with me, Turner," Hans said. "I know you're stronger than me. There's no denying you're younger. And those ruthless looks might get you far in business dealings, but you can't intimidate me. I know you too well."

"Care to tell me what this is about?" Turner said.

"I know your father died."

Jolted, Turner said, "How? I've never spoken of my family. No one knows who my father is."

"I'm not an idiot, son. T.D. Brockman was well known in the international business world. The infamous 'soulless' Brockman brought down in an instant by a heart attack. I can only imagine what your childhood was like. I see how detached you are. Not getting close to anyone. Melanie and I feel lucky you've shared what you have with us over the years."

"You've been good to me," Turner began, struggling to find his words. "But I can't go back. Not now. I don't know if I ever can."

"You will. Even if only to blast through the ghosts and get on with your life. It's obvious you're not sleeping. You're being an asshole to your staff. And if you snap at your secretary one more time, she's liable to quit. Face the past, Turner. It will eat away at you if you don't. You'll find your e-ticket in your email."

"You're my boss, not my father," Turner said, the steel in his voice matching his eyes. One last attempt to deflect.

"I'm your friend, you idiot. And I care about you."

One sentence was all it took to deflate Turner's temper. Hans was one of the only friends Turner had. He ran his hands through his hair and sighed. God, he felt fifty pounds heavier. It was a struggle to stay awake at his desk. Even work couldn't keep the memories at bay.

"I don't know if I can." Deep inside, a coil of fear tightened in his chest, but that was something he wouldn't admit to anyone. He'd spent years putting distance between himself and Graciella, between himself and the people he loved. Every step he'd climbed had been with the intention of banishing his past. All of it. Including the bond with his brothers and the love for his mother, because he'd let them all down. Because the truth was, even though he'd finally grown to hate T.D., as a child he'd craved the man's approval, wanted to be just like him. How sick was that? It wasn't only memories of T.D. he ran from, it was his own shame in loving his father. He'd loved a tyrant, longed for his love in return. How could he ever reconcile that?

"You can and you will. Your flight leaves tonight at seven." Hans busied himself with his papers. "Your job will be here when you return. Now I'm late for a meeting." He smiled and strode out of the office. Even with the friendship they'd formed over the years, Turner knew when Hans meant business.

Hell! Turner thought, closing his eyes to the memories trying to purge themselves from his gut. Fine. He'd go back to Graciella, confront his ghosts, try to apologize. Then move on to the next development deal up the ladder in his career. A career that had never disappointed him...at least where power and money were concerned.

Chapter Two

For most people Sunday was a day of rest. Lily didn't believe in rest, but her job sites were closed on Sundays. They were on Saturdays too when business was slow and her crew wanted the day off. But since she'd returned to Graciella, there'd been no such thing as slow. *Perfect*. The busier, the better. The more projects she got to juggle, the more thrilling life was for her. Like the finale of fireworks lighting up the sky, a million brilliant designs sparked through her mind and fingers together. It matched her energy. And it was thrilling to own her own company and be able to call the shots. On Sundays, she had only one commitment—to herself—but that didn't mean she slowed down.

The promise of a clear, sunny day stretched ahead of her, despite the chilly morning breeze ruffling the air. *Ah, the Graciella sea air.* She breathed it in deeply. "Home," it said to her, energy and belonging in one blast. Every morning this summer, weather allowing, she started her day swimming the length of her very own backyard pool. She'd finished the landscaping in April, and it was her favorite place in the world. Okay, second favorite place. Hmm, she could probably name at least ten favorite places, but this pool rocked. Sparkling blue water surrounded by lush, scented flora. Wild roses bloomed. Still young, they would eventually climb up the fences. Lavender was bursting into flower, and jasmine lined the back of her house. Even the sweet peas sent perfume into the air with each new, fragile bloom. She loved how delicate, yet powerful those blossoms were.

The water refreshed and energized her. With each lap she drew her body and mind into a meditative state and cleared the never-ending chatter in her head. Stroke after stroke. Her arms sliced through the water, pulling her strong body forward. It was the beginning to a perfect day. Sundays she worked on her special project without being needed at any of her other job sites or feeling guilty because she wasn't there. After finishing her laps, she floated and watched the puffy white clouds dance across the Graciella sky.

My job sites. She loved the sound of that. Little Lily Moreno, once scrawny and awkward, now owned her own business in what was traditionally a man's domain, construction and restoration. She could laugh at the number of times people had opened their jaws in shock when she told them what she did. Either that or they flat out didn't believe her.

After a quick shower, Liliana grabbed coffee, a package of cold strawberry Pop Tarts, and drove slowly into downtown Graciella. Her truck made more noises than a cranky old man. Well, it *was* cranky and ancient, but she loved it and was too stubborn to get a new one. A new one would just get dusty and dirty.

She hadn't gone into construction for the shock value or to prove anything to anyone. It was her passion. Lily loved to build things with her hands, to carve out of the figurative stone and create lasting impressions, often restoring grand old beauties others had tossed aside. She married the past to the present and hoped the quality of her work would carry her projects into the future.

As a bonus, she'd found the perfect place to build. Her research and study had taken her adventuring for a few years, but now she was back in Graciella where she belonged. Where she had the perfect balance of work, beautiful land and family. And now that the cruel landowner T.D. Brockman was dead, maybe Lily could finally help awaken this wonderful town from its fearful slumber.

Lily believed in fate and timing and she felt it was Graciella's time to bloom, just like her garden of flowers. Her passion was on fire and she was completely in control of her life and the path she'd carved. And that path included her beloved hometown.

She snaked her truck through the construction signs and orange barrels from the road crew that was working on Main Street during the week and parked at an angle that would make getting the long boards of wood out of her truck and straight into the theater easier. Lily put her earbuds in, cranked up Brandi Carlile and got to work.

Brandi was in the middle of an angsty love song when the two by fours Lily carried over her shoulder smacked against something behind her.

"Holy hell!" she swore as the impact jarred her. When she turned to inspect what had gotten in her way, her heart flipped over. Not something, someone.

No. No. No! It can't be. Not here. Not now. Not ever. She slammed the wood to the ground and sucked in a breath. Turner Brockman in the flesh. Lily ripped out her earbuds, her music replaced with a shadow from the past.

"I'll second that," he said, rubbing his shoulder. She followed the motion of his arm. She'd smacked *him* with her two by fours. *Appropriate.* His voice was deeper, but, even with his pissy tone, she'd recognize the sound anywhere.

"I didn't see you…" *No one's seen you in twelve years.* Her heart hovered and fluttered in recognition. *Oh, no you don't, you traitor. We do not love him anymore.*

"See me? What about hear me?" he said, his voice edged with cold annoyance. "You left your truck blocking the road. I honked at you, twice. What kind of an idiot leaves his truck in the middle of the street full of lumber in broad daylight?"

Lily's shock and surprise flipped over into anger. *Idiot? Honked at me? 'His' truck?* Oh, hell no! She wasn't prepared for his return. She'd told herself he never would. It was the only way to exist, to move on once she'd picked up the shattered pieces of her young heart. Oh, how naïve she'd been. Thank goodness she'd grown up.

He stood there lecturing and thinking she was a *man*. *Why* had she ever fallen for him? *Jesus*, he didn't even recognize her. She'd often wondered what kind of an impression she'd made on him. Now she knew — absolutely none. The jerk he'd been as a teenager seemed to have exploded into its full identity. And he was in her face. *Great! Just fricking great!*

She turned and stalked outside. *Just who's the idiot?* She made it to her truck and could hear Turner yelling after her. She dug in the bed of her pickup for her toolbox and tried to regulate her breathing. Seeing Turner had knocked it loose and it skimmed and fizzed out of control, like scrambling to find breath after diving into freezing water.

Turner Duke Brockman, middle and favored of the three Brockman sons. The one who'd been gone for over a decade now. She should know — she'd never forgotten the day he left, or everything that had happened before he'd deserted them all. Or how much she'd loved him once. Her first love, so much more than a crush, and it had taken her years to get over him. But she had gotten over her feelings. Or, rather, shoved them to the pit of her stomach, where they could stay hidden, burning in acid.

At least she'd thought so, until she'd been lasered by his sharp sage eyes again. Adrenaline raced through her. She wanted to vomit, but there was no way on this earth she would let him see how affected she was. He hadn't known she loved him then, and she wouldn't allow him that leverage over her now.

"Maybe you don't have any manners." Turner stormed out of the building. "But I'm sure your employer wouldn't like to hear that you left your truck blocking traffic."

"My employer?" Lily's hackles shot up. *Yes, find the wrench so you can smack him upside the head with it.* Probably not the best idea since her hand was shaking. Good Lord. Turner, here, in Graciella.

"As in your boss. It's dangerous. Perhaps he doesn't give you proper regulations for work."

God, the condescending tone was enough to have her eyes roll back so hard they stuck. "Dangerous? Regulations?" He was a pompous ass. That she could deal with. Matching his anger, she ignored the fact that his eyes, even when angry, could still melt her heart.

Turner paused and ran his hand over his face in frustration. "Maybe you don't understand me."

Her own temper flared. "Oh, I understand *you* perfectly." She poked him in the chest. "Everything you've yelled at me since you arrived. 'What kind of idiot leaves *his* car in the middle of the road?' Well, let's see." Liliana took off her cap, letting her curls tumble around her face. "The kind of idiot who can't read the signs — 'Detour — construction vehicles only — all other traffic take Mission Street' — I believe, Turner Brockman."

She pointed at the black sports car he'd left sitting in the road with the door hanging open. "That idiot would be you. Welcome home. It's nice of you to grace us with your presence after all these years." Liliana tossed her head back, pushed him out of the way and drove off, leaving the only man who could ever hurt her standing in the dust.

Turner blinked and tried to understand what had happened. A rage-filled punk rock band drummed a horrible song in his head, beat after relentless beat. Sun, which should have made him happy, overheated his weathered, hungover and dehydrated body. A few splinters stuck out of his hand, mixed with dried blood, and one pissed-off woman had just railed at him. A woman, and not a boy in a Yankees cap, like he'd originally assumed when he'd watched him, no, *her* carry boards into the old theater. Not even close.

He'd been put in his place. And if he hadn't been so annoyed and embarrassed, he might have been impressed by the way she'd done it.

A woman he'd never seen before knew exactly who he was and that he hadn't been home in many long years. *Welcome home indeed.* He hadn't even made it to the farm and already this trip was a disaster. Exhausted after the ten-hour flight from Berlin to Portland, then another short flight to the small airstrip an hour from Graciella, he'd driven through downtown on autopilot, where a woman with fiery eyes had singed him and sliced him right to his guilt.

Maybe the rest of them would let him sleep for a few years before they added to her anger. He could handle a regular fight with words and fists if he had to. Hell, he was expecting one from his family.

Driving to Brockman Farms was torture, but he'd told no one he was coming and there was no other way, save walking the seventy miles. The rhythm of the car's movement matched the throbbing pain in his head. Turner slowed the car when the street stretched out into rolling farmlands. Each curve of the winding roads stirred his stomach and the contents threatened to surge up his throat.

Other than him feeling like death warmed over, it was a gorgeous day in the Pacific Northwest, a place he'd once believed was better than any on earth. With a cobalt sky and a scent in the air that many claimed was due to a perfect blend of saltwater, fresh clean life and pine trees after a brilliant spring storm. Water, mountains, rugged land and rocky cliffs, this region held everything. *For some.* For him, the salty sea air brought forth T.D.'s image, his father's cruel eyes that had haunted Turner for too long.

Unexpectedly, it also shook loose a whole lot more. With one scent, his emotions were in upheaval. Memories swirled around him, not all of them the brutal ones he'd tried to bury. Happy memories surrounded him too. Riding bikes with his brothers along the crops, trying to outrace each other. Diving in and out of the surf on windy days. Planting seedlings with his mother in her garden.

He'd told himself he'd come to Graciella and make amends where he was able, destroy the hold his father had on him. Then he'd return to Berlin. Instead, he felt like a recovered addict falling off the wagon. The summer air had bled right into him like a craving. A love, a desire long buried hit him in the chest. He'd once loved this place. He'd once loved the people. He'd once *belonged* here.

Chapter Three

Lily ignored the urge to look in her rearview mirror. She rolled down her windows and hoped a cool breeze would reach her. But there was no such thing now on this scorching afternoon, more like a hot desert wind that whipped her hair into her eyes. She was sweaty and dirty and, thanks to one uptight jerk, could now add angry to that combination. And curious…how stupid to be curious. Twelve years ago, her heart had found its mate. But his had never reciprocated. He'd never even seen her. The whole thing was so humiliating, and painful to remember, but she doubted she'd ever forget any of it, how he'd hurt her or the pain of him leaving. Or how it had felt to love him, like flying. Like clouds and dreams and the sun warming her skin.

What the hell was he doing back now? She'd heard a little about him in recent years, mostly from the business pages of the international newspapers. It was impossible *not* to read about him. The man helped run one of the largest development firms in Europe — he played with the big boys.

And, after all this time, he was still an obnoxious, self-righteous brat. She huffed and powered her truck up the hills.

There were moments in her secret dreams when she still wondered about him. She had imagined what he might look like as he'd grown from the boy she remembered. How her name might sound on his lips. If the scent of his skin was intoxicating. But she hadn't believed he would ever return to Graciella. He hadn't, after all, in twelve years. Not once. He'd walked away from his home and his family without a backward glance, which Lily could never understand because she'd seen how much he loved them, and how that love was returned to him.

Personally, she'd never been one to squander love, which was why she doled it out to her friends and family in limitless supply. And also why, after Turner left, she'd never trusted a man with her heart. *Never.*

Why now, Turner? We've all moved on without you. "Shit!" She smacked the steering wheel. He was the new owner of T.D.'s properties and the farmhouse and workers' cottages right here in Graciella. Valuable properties, every single one. To those in Graciella, their value was in the legacy, the town. To an outsider, the value would be in dollar signs. What would Turner see in them? And what would he do with them? Obliterate them, like he had his past? And here she was tangled up in every single property, professionally and personally.

More questions flared through Lily's mind, but she tried to ignore them and the worries they stirred in both her business concerns and her soul. She didn't have time for an imbecile like Turner Brockman to distract her. Her work in town was finished, but her day wasn't over. Even though the nurses at the home took wonderful care of her papá, and even though Lily was unrecognizable to him now that he had Alzheimer's, she visited him a few times every week.

Mentally, to regain her cool before she checked in on him, Lily itemized her to-do list for the week. *Finish custom doors for the old train station that's being refurbished. Order windows for clients on Baker Street. And, this evening, check out the progress on the new section of Brockman House.*

Liliana sighed. Ignoring anything Brockman-related was useless. Such a strange and tangled relationship she'd had with the Brockmans over the years. First there was T.D., the meanest man she'd ever met. Before his death, it had seemed he'd nearly owned the entire town. He'd certainly ruled over it, with the massive farm that employed so many, and his attempts to buy all the properties downtown.

Many of the families in Graciella had come for the place's beauty. Some had drifted up from California, after crossing the border from Mexico to look for work, others from busy American cities, seeking fresh air and land. Explorers from faraway countries had built up this grand old town. People had come seeking a better life for themselves and their families. Her mother and father, first-generation Spanish Americans, had run the hardware store and the one-screen theater in the small downtown. Two buildings T.D. hadn't been able to get his hands on until last year, when her father's health had rapidly deteriorated. Right before Lily had returned, her father had sold the hardware store to T.D. in what Liliana still believed was a real estate deal that lacked ethics, if not legality.

With the cruel Brockman patriarch dead, she'd hoped there would be some clarity, but T.D.'s estate was proving to be as menacing and miserable to understand as the man had been. One morning a few weeks ago, the empty buildings everyone thought T.D. had purchased over the years had displayed Premier Realtors signs. The entire thing was an annoying stitch in her side that she couldn't get rid of. Cruz, the oldest Brockman brother, executor of T.D.'s holdings, had been digging through layers of confusion for months, trying to understand it all. His fiancée, Miranda, and his lawyer had been helping, but answers eluded them. The complicated mess had added to the nightmare of getting the estate fully settled.

I still have the theater. Lily breathed a deep sigh of gratitude. If losing the hardware store meant Lily got to keep the theater, she would try to find contentment with that. Her father had run the hardware store for profit and the theater for love.

Liliana still remembered watching her mother's face light up every time a movie came onto the screen in the darkened theater. Even after her mother died when Liliana was twelve, her father kept both businesses going, until a few years ago.

Katie Brockman, mother to Cruz, Turner and Adam, had been the one to finally call her and tell her something wasn't right. The diagnosis had come quickly once Lily had gotten him to the doctor for tests. They'd discovered his Alzheimer's in the later stages. That guilt ate at her. He'd been suffering and losing himself all alone, while she'd been falling in love with the world.

She'd come home to find her father sick and the theater closed and empty. It stood ghostlike, had been closed for years, fallen on hard times as the economy roller-coastered its way through small towns and as its owner slowly lost the ability to care for it.

At first Lily intended to reopen it, but seeing the layer of dust and hovering memories, she decided that wasn't enough for such a grand structure. She could feel it in her veins. Her theater was a beautiful lady, fallen on hard times, ready to make a comeback. She deserved more than a little love and care. She deserved to shine. *Fancy makeup, a whole new wardrobe. One stunning makeover.* Lily didn't do anything halfway and once she'd gotten the bug to fix up the place, she'd decided on glamorous. Oh, yes, her theater was going to light up the town, the way she'd always been meant to do. Refurbishing the theater was her baby, a selfish one, she knew, but she didn't care. It was worth all the long, extra hours of working alone to completely revitalize it.

Lily had created over thirty jobs with her construction company. There would be more once the café, artisan gallery and B & B at Brockman Farms were up and running. People would rediscover Graciella's paradise. They'd come for the jobs and stay for the beauty and the amenities. The town was blooming and she intended for the theater to be the brightest flower in the center of it all.

Katie Brockman had been by a few times to help clean out the mess left by all the years of neglect. Katie couldn't have been more different from T.D. Where T.D. had been cruel and cold, Katie showed compassion and kindness for everyone she met.

Then there were the Brockman brothers. Closer to Adam's age, she'd spent most of her time playing with him, and he'd always been like a little brother to her. Cruz had mostly teased her when they were growing up, and the one she wished she could forget about was Turner.

Quiet, guarded Turner. He hadn't always been an egotistical jerk. She'd been in awe of him. Of his strength, his fierce looks. Turner could outrun anyone. He swam like a dolphin. And once he started high school, the coaches were duking it out to get him on their team. He used to tell ghost stories up in the rafters of the barn to his brothers and her, sometimes Miguel and Roxanna too. He took care of them, made them laugh, and he protected them. Eventually, her awe had sparked a full-blown crush.

It had started the summer she turned fifteen. Turner had grown so tall and his voice had changed, and she couldn't quit looking at him, hoping that he'd gaze at her with those intense eyes. Eyes that always seemed to be hiding deep secrets. Secrets she wanted to believe he would tell only her.

But he hadn't shared any secrets with her. He'd barely acknowledged her. And he'd certainly never gotten close enough to touch her. Instead he'd squashed her heart like a bug when she was seventeen. A moment she wished she could forget forever and the only regret she ever had.

It wasn't long after that horrible day that Turner, star athlete, had quit his sports — football, baseball, track…he'd simply walked away from all of them. And once he'd quit, he'd completely withdrawn into himself.

She'd once thought him gorgeous, swoony.

Still gorgeous. A gorgeous jackass dressed in his fancy business clothes. She rounded the curve leading up to her father's nursing home. Thank goodness she was stronger and wiser. What she'd felt back then might have been her first love, but really it was also an ignorant girl's ridiculous ideals of the world. Turner's only thought of her back then was that she was stupid and weak. Her first love wasted on an idiot. Holy crap, it had bruised her young heart.

Putting away her old pains, Liliana quietly found her way to her father's room. It was awash in light, which made her happy. The nursing home had been transformed from an old furniture store and many of the large windows still remained, adding a bit of hope to an otherwise hushed and sad place. She'd filled his room with the succulents he'd loved and babied, and the new television sat next to a collection of DVDs. She'd purchased an oversized cushy loveseat and ottoman for him, so they could curl up together and watch movies, but that phase hadn't lasted long. He slept more than he was awake these days.

This afternoon he slept again and she kicked herself. Partly it was guilt that ate at her for not being here more often when he was awake, and partly she knew it was selfish of her to want that. He was so peaceful when he slept. The lines of confusion that marred his forehead smoothed out into gentleness, and he wasn't agitated with everything he no longer knew or remembered.

She climbed into the chair by his bed and picked up *The River Why* by David James Duncan, one of her father's favorite novels and one that calmed her too with its beauty. But while she sat in the sunlight, she couldn't fully still the churning in her heart. Memories of her youth with her papá, the father he used to be, strong and intelligent, both father and mother to her after her mother's death, beat at her. Threaded throughout were images of Turner and Brockman Farms. Change was here. She felt it like a rumble of a small earthquake, a nudge of greater things to come, and worse, happenings she felt she'd have no control over.

Liliana wiped the exhaustion from her face and with it the memories and wishes assaulting her. As the owner of the thriving Dragonfly Design Construction & Fine Woodworking, she had precious little time to waste contemplating the past.

The present was its own beast to battle.

Now one insulting, *handsome* idiot from her past was back. *Why does he have to be so damned good-looking?*

Those steely green eyes of Turner Brockman seared into her mind and opened the floodgates to her questions. *What's he doing back? How long before he runs away again? How will his presence affect the new construction at Brockman House and all the Graciella properties he now owns?* Most importantly, could she keep her heart wrapped up tight and protected? She'd never been able to where he was concerned. But twelve years was a long time to build that wall. There was no way she'd let herself get close again.

Lily lived and loved freely and wildly. Keeping her emotions under the radar wasn't something she was good at or enjoyed. But for survival? Well, she could do anything for survival.

Chapter Four

Two things stood out on Turner's first glimpse of the main house at Brockman Farms. The first was the construction crew remodeling one huge side of it. From a brief phone conversation with his brothers about the will, Turner knew they had plans to turn Brockman House into an inn or a destination of sorts. He hadn't listened to the details and hadn't much cared more than to give his consent.

The shock that had consumed him since the news of T.D.'s death was a shield between him and his brothers. *They* spoke about the future. Happiness and hope poured out with their words. And he was sleepwalking through a dark tunnel. Now, seeing the place he'd been afraid of for more than a decade, the reality slammed into him. T.D. Brockman was gone. For good.

The entire north wing was being rebuilt. A rough frame was already up. It looked amazing from Turner's viewpoint. He'd never seen this many people at the main house at once, humming with positive energy. It was alive. It forced Turner to see the grand house and farmland in a different way. And thank Christ for that. He took some deep breaths and focused on the changes, the new.

It was the second thing that awed him more. His mother, emboldened under the sun. She fed lunch to the construction crew at long picnic tables that had been set up on the front lawn. Katie Brockman dished out ribs and corn, laughed and joked with the workers. She was smiling. That was a memory Turner had never forgotten, the warmth of his mother's smile. Under the shroud of T.D., his mother had always had a smile for him, but he'd seen her hide her warmth so often. *Not anymore.*

He hoped his homecoming wouldn't make her too angry. Turner parked and walked toward the tables.

As if sensing him, his mom looked up. She blinked for an instant. Her smile didn't disappear, as he'd thought it might. Instead she stretched out her arms and said, "Oh, my goodness. Turner."

"Mom..." Words stuck like molasses in his throat. He'd become a pro at avoiding emotion.

"I knew you'd come home." She tightened her hold.

Home? All these years he'd stayed away and still she had such faith in him. He didn't even know the meaning of home.

Guilt ate at him. Never glancing backward, only keeping loose tabs on the farm through Adam and Cruz over the years because his brothers had made the effort to keep in touch.

"Mom. You're more beautiful than ever."

"And I'm even happier now that I have all my boys home."

Jesus Christ. He felt off balance in the sweltering sun. Or under the weight of his guilt?

"God dammit! Turner!" Adam, his younger brother, tackled Turner in a hug.

Adam's enthusiasm and size busted a laugh out of Turner. God, it felt good to see his family. He hadn't anticipated any of this, smiles, warmth, hugs. He hadn't realized how much he needed it, this care and love. How something as elementary as a hug felt like soothing away all the open scars he'd nursed for so long by himself.

"What the hell happened to my baby brother?" No longer the scrawny kid Turner had tried to protect from T.D.'s wrath, Adam had outgrown them all. *Like a bull at a rodeo.* Powerful, strong, scary, in contrast to the huge grin on his freckled, tan face.

"Wait till you see everything that's going on around here. And you'd better stay for the wedding. Shock the hell out of Cruz. I knew you'd get here. This is where we belong. Together."

Belong? "Wedding?" Turner choked out.

"Cruz and Miranda. You'll meet her soon. She's around here somewhere. Probably tweaking the café designs. Look, I'll see you later for dinner. I've got supplies to unload." And quicker than he'd blown in, Adam was climbing into his truck and heading down the road.

"I guess I have been gone a long time," Turner said quietly.

"He's not a kid anymore. None of you are." Katie's voice was softer, serious. She focused on Turner. "A lot has happened since you left. You don't have to be afraid anymore."

Her words reached into his fears and jump-started his heart. She had every right to withhold her forgiveness. But, Christ, this open acceptance was a balm.

"You can stay here at the house or in the red cottage. Wherever you're comfortable." Her words broke him out of his reverie.

He hadn't given a second thought to where he'd stay once he arrived. Getting here had taken most of his energy and apparently most of his brain cells. *Stay at Brockman House?* Would the ghosts eat him alive? He'd be damned if he'd let them. He looked at the gentle love and happiness in her eyes. "I'll stay in the house. If that's all right with you?"

"It hasn't been my home for years, Turner. And besides, it belongs to you now. Head inside. Elena's in the kitchen. She'll get a room ready for you. Have a nice shower and get some sleep. You look like you could use it."

How could they make it so easy on him? Why hadn't they yelled at him, accused him, lashed out over his epic absence? He'd misjudged them and their reactions to his homecoming. Jesus, homecoming! Now *he* was using the word. This was not his home. He hated the place. At least he'd told himself he did. Over and over, for so long, trying to make himself believe it.

Maybe Hans was right—maybe it would do him good to put his ghosts to rest. What did that really mean? Being back here now, he felt like he was searching for something too. Absolution, perhaps, or more? What *more* could there be for him in Graciella? Everything he'd encountered so far, the ocean breeze, hugs from his mother and brother, the fiery temper of the woman who'd yelled at him in town, roused his senses. Restlessness stirred inside him and with it a sort of loosening of the fist around his gut.

Chapter Five

Turner slept like a dead man. He wasn't sure what felt better, the first nightmare-less sleep he'd had in weeks or the hot, hard shower he stood under now. *Thank God for good water pressure.* He washed away the sweat and a mixture of alcohol and airplane staleness from his body. One last thing he needed was coffee, desperately. What were the chances he'd find an espresso maker in the kitchen?

As he wandered from the south wing and stepped onto the landing dividing it from the north, his senses picked up more changes around the once cold, dark Brockman House. The first was noise. From the new north wing, with its frame construction and windows still without glass, came the sounds of saws, drills and boards being nailed into place. Seagulls bickered overhead and a quick blast of wind shook leaves into a flutter. People's voices, loud and confident, soared through it all. From downstairs came music and laughter.

Nothing could have shocked him more. Laughter and music in the Brockman House? *Am I still asleep?*

He also nearly fainted at the scent of grilled salmon, garlic and spices drifting up. And, if his nose told him right, coffee. Whether dreaming or not, he decided to let his stomach lead the way into the kitchen where he was faced with another unusual sight. His mother, Katie, laughing and dancing with an intense-looking man dressed in black from his T-shirt and jeans to old worn-in cowboy boots. Black hair streaked with silver was tied in a ponytail at the base of his neck. Although he was casually dressed, there was nothing casual about his presence. There was nothing casual about the way he looked at Katie either.

Adam had told him about Javier. Katie had fallen in love with and forfeited all of Brockman Farms for Javier. Leaving T.D. meant giving up her birthright, the land that had been in her family for generations. Together, Katie and Javier, even in the face of T.D.'s power, had secretly continued to help the people around them.

Unlike Javier, a good, brave man, Turner had run. And aside from his boss and mentor, Hans, Turner had eschewed personal connections at every chance. Once he'd tasted the confusion and fear of being close to people—those he loved but couldn't protect, and the one man he'd wanted love from who would never give it—he'd never wanted a sip of it again. Being close to people meant he could be hurt, or, worse, hurt them.

Shaken, he grabbed the door frame to steady himself. In order to leave the real ghosts behind, he knew he'd have to make amends for his own wrongs.

Evening sunlight poured in through the east-facing windows. Louis Armstrong came from the antique record player. Javier twirled his mother, barefoot with her floral apron tied around her waist, on the hardwood floors.

Javier saw Turner and, never missing a step, winked at him, dipped his mother to her delight and surprise, then brought her back up and kissed her.

They fit well together. He couldn't help but relax and smile. "Bravo." Turner clapped.

Katie laughed. "We were wondering if you were ever going to wake up. Would you like some coffee?" She reached for a mug.

"You read my mind, Mom. You must be Javier." Turner reached his hand out.

"It's nice to finally meet you, Turner. It's good you came home. Many people around here missed you." Without hesitation, the older man grabbed Turner in a strong embrace and said, "I'm going to check on the grill." It took Turner a moment to recover from the onslaught of emotions that kept rolling over him.

"Mom." He leaned against the counter by her. "You're happy."

She stopped what she was doing and looked directly at him. A youthful flush crept into her cheeks. "Yes."

"I'm happy for you."

Her eyes were glassy with tears, even while she laughed. "I don't even know where these tears came from. I think I was worried you'd be angry."

"I'm angry at myself. I need to apologize to you. The things I said to you before I left. The *way* I left...I—"

"You were upset," Katie said, straightforward now. "You had every right to be. As hard as I tried, I could never protect you boys enough from T.D. And for that I'll always feel shame. There were things I couldn't explain to you at that point. Then you were gone and it seemed better to let you lead your life free from any more baggage."

"I walked out on you and everyone. Don't you want to yell at me?"

"You were a boy with too much on your shoulders. I should have told you why I stayed with T.D. At first, out of fear that he'd take you boys from me, and later to help the workers. I'll always regret that I didn't get a chance to before you left, but you had to get away from here, from him." She paused for a minute. "I spent too many years regretting the past. It's a horrible way to live. You're home and that's all that matters." She put the tableware down and hugged him again.

He hadn't anticipated how many hugs would be so easily tossed his way, or how they might, little by little, ease his worries, warm his frozen heart. He leaned back on the counter and took in the kitchen. The evening light softened everything and gave it a comfortable welcome feeling.

Well, so much for easy. His relaxation didn't last long. *Here comes the chewing-out I deserve.* Cruz stood in the doorway. They faced each other in silence. Shock or anger washed over Cruz's face. Turner couldn't tell. He was ashamed to realize his brother had become a stranger to him.

"When did you get here?" Cruz asked.

"A few hours ago."

"Why now...? I don't..." Cruz struggled with his words and oddly enough it was the break Turner needed.

He shrugged and said, "I'm not sure. Fuck, I don't know what I'm doing, Cruz. But it's good to see you."

"Javier says two platters, one for the salmon and one for..." A woman rounded the corner next to Cruz. "Oh, you must be Turner." She placed her hand on his arm and said, "I'm Miranda."

Her light touch broke his gaze from Cruz's. "Adam mentioned Cruz'd gotten himself attached. He said you were beautiful. He was right."

Miranda laughed. "Handsome and a charmer."

"Miranda, help me take these platters to Javier," Katie said.

"Good idea. Dinner's almost ready. Don't take too long reuniting or there might not be any food left."

Where the noise had shocked Turner before, now it was the quiet. A painful, stressful silence coiled taut between them, full of so much that had never been spoken, haunting them.

"I know why you had to leave here. God, I was the same, but to completely shut me out for the past, I don't even know how many years it's been."

"I'm sorry. I don't even know what to say. I thought if I...I just shoved everything into some dark place. For a while it became easier, until it—" The weight of it all, the past, his regrets, the present threatened to flatten him.

"Until what?" The anger had bled away from Cruz's expression.

"Until it all surged up again. Every damn day. In my nightmares."

Cruz took a few moments to study him, then finally put his hand out. "I get it. It's good to see you too."

"It's been..." Turner took the outstretched hand and could still feel a reserve between them. No friendly hugs here. "Too long." He forced the words out, his explanation, his crappy attempt at apology. How did one begin to apologize for who he was at his core, especially when everyone was making it so easy for him to be here, to just be? "A lot's happened."

"Yes," Cruz replied.

"Place looks amazing. I'd like to hear about everything from you." God, where did he begin? He'd built thirty-story high-rises. He spoke five languages, charmed his way through disastrous business meetings and empty affairs. But now, here he was, a naïve coward.

"We'll talk later." Cruz seemed to relax with Turner's uncomfortableness. "Katie and Javier have a feast ready outside. Everyone's here. They want to see you. I'm glad you're home, Turner." Cruz gave a small grin and smacked him on the shoulder.

"Look who I found loitering around out front." Adam's voice came from the doorway, his arm around a woman's shoulders. A gorgeous stunner of a woman. Recognition slammed into Turner. The woman from the construction site earlier. No longer dressed in jeans and a work shirt. Instead she wore a simple summer dress in iridescent browns. Sleeveless, it skimmed over her body, swayed out from her waist and rested above her knees.

Nothing simple about that dress, or her. He tried to swallow, but found his throat blanched dry. Gorgeous brown hair shimmered with streaks of deep red and gold. Curls framed her face, leaving her shoulders bare. Soft, glowing shoulders. Her skin radiated like she'd dusted on glitter. Endless legs drew his gaze all the way down to her toes peeking out from copper-colored sandals. Then there was her scent, a scent that shot straight to his gut, like jasmine on a hot summer's night. He must have been blind this morning to have mistaken her for a boy.

She'd bewitched him and he wasn't quite sure she was a friendly witch. Sparks of fire shot from her eyes, aimed directly at him.

"You remember Liliana, don't you, Turner?" Adam said.

"I…" The dryness crept into his mouth.

"We reacquainted ourselves this afternoon." Liliana glared at Turner.

"We… I…" Turner couldn't seem to form more than one word.

"Hey, beautiful. Staying for dinner?" Cruz asked.

"She's trying to get out of it," Adam said. "Tried to tell me she wasn't hungry. Ha, good thing we know her obsession with food. I told her once everyone knew she was here, they wouldn't let her leave. Javier caught the salmon this morning, Turner's home, Miguel and Roxanna brought the kids. Family dinner with all of us finally together again. You're family, Lily. You guys coming?" Adam propelled Liliana out to the back yard.

"You look stunned." Cruz elbowed Turner in the gut and grabbed several wine bottles.

"I…"

Cruz laughed. "You said that already. Come on. Like you said, a lot's changed."

Chapter Six

Lily knew the moment Turner came outside. Even with her back to him, his presence filled her senses. She and Miranda were laughing at little Serafina, Roxanna and Miguel's newest baby. All nine pounds of her had just finished spitting up on Miguel.

"You'd think a man would get used to this after all the times it's happened." Miguel spoke directly to Serafina and wiped the spit off his shirt. "It's a good thing you're beautiful like your mother. It's hard to be mad at you, little one."

"I thought I was beautiful?" Ana, almost nine years old, said in her singsong voice to Miguel.

"You are, Ana Banana. All my women are beautiful."

"Damn, Turner! We thought you'd never come home!" Miguel said.

"Watch your language," Roxanna shushed him, but she was smiling, happiness radiating from her. She and

Miguel seemed more in love now than when they were teenagers.

Lily shouldn't have come here tonight. She'd told herself she needed to check on the progress of the new construction, but she'd showered and put on a dress plus the perfect seductive hint of makeup and scent in case she ran into Turner. She wanted to drive him crazy, annoyed that the first time he'd seen her after all these years she'd been dressed in old work clothes and baseball hat that had seen too many decades. *Covered in sawdust and wood stain and sweaty – how dare he not recognize me!*

She hadn't planned on Adam dragging her back to eat dinner with the family. Normally, she felt at home and at ease surrounded by this group of wonderful people. Tonight, the air heavy with old love and new love made her feel out of place and fidgety. Miguel and Roxanna, Katie and Javier, and one had to be dead not to notice how in love Miranda and Cruz were. Lily gazed around and sadness clawed at her heart. A rarity for her. Sad wasn't a comfortable place for Lily. When that lonely emotion did manage to sneak up on her, she put her energy into making things. Right now, all she had was the wineglass in her hand to toy with.

Lily wandered over to the grill where Javier tended to the salmon and asparagus. She picked up the tongs, turned the vegetables and tried to focus on someone else besides the ache inside her, besides the presence of ghosts. "You look happy, Javier." She nudged him.

The man had led a difficult life. He'd spent the last decade working for T.D., but really taking care of the migrant workers. Where some might have turned bitter and angry, Javier had always been steady and strong. He'd swept Katie off her feet right after Turner had left for college. If she'd ever seen honor embodied by a man, it was Javier. He exuded a wonderful mix of wisdom and humor. Now he practically glowed with happiness.

Javier kissed her on the cheek. "And you look beautiful. So…" He paused and basted the fish with a glaze. "How are you?"

Besides Roxanna, Javier was the only one who'd known all those years ago how she'd felt about Turner. He'd found her hiding in the barn one day, sobbing, a week after Turner had left Graciella without saying goodbye. When he'd found her, she'd been so overcome with heartbreak, she'd blurted out everything. Afterward she'd felt humiliated, a stupid little girl dramatizing something into more than it really was. But he'd never made fun of her or discounted her feelings. Instead he'd said to her, *'Love is never something to be ashamed of, even when it hurts you.'*

"Fine," she said now, ignoring his eyes.

"Perhaps you'd better tell the asparagus you're not here to murder them."

She paused. She'd been flipping the asparagus over with enough force to shred them. Two had fallen between the grill grates.

"It doesn't go away that easily," he said and gently took the tongs from her hand.

"What doesn't?"

"Love."

"What are you talking about? I'm not in love." She fumed and grabbed the tongs back, but refrained from committing any more vegetable murder.

"I can see that." Javier laughed

"How ridiculous. He's been gone for, what, eight years?" *Twelve.* "Anyway, it wasn't love to begin with.

It was a crush, foolish and unreciprocated." *It was everything. And humiliating.*

Javier stopped laughing and looked at her with those wonderful, wise old eyes, "I told you once, love is never something to be ashamed of. Especially your one true love. Time is the only ridiculous thing when it comes to the heart. Time is immeasurable, irrelevant. Time means nothing if the love is real." His voice was serious, and he held her gaze.

He had a way of teaching her things without making her feel stupid, but this time, Liliana wasn't so sure he was right. *My one true love? He didn't even remember me.* She wanted to cry.

"Ahh, Turner," Javier began. "Just in time to help us with the salmon. You hold the platter and I'll take it off the grill."

"Liliana," Turner said, looking at her while Javier loaded up the salmon.

She glared at him, more unsettled now than when she arrived. He looked even better than before, rested, in a casual shirt and jeans and meeting her gaze, sharp and curious. Damn him for looking so good in dressy business attire *and* random jeans and wrinkled T-shirt. *Bet he looks better naked.* Good God, where had that thought come from? And along with it, heat and embarrassment flooded her cheeks. She took a long drink of her chilled white wine and, without saying anything, walked away.

* * * *

Dinner put Liliana on edge. She knew it was because of Turner. She felt completely at home at the Brockman House, but not tonight. Even though he'd been gone for so long, it was his home, not hers. More so now that his name was on the deed. He'd hardly spoken at dinner, but she'd caught him stealing glances at her. *Good. Look all you want, Turner.* But she couldn't deny the jittery feelings his gaze stirred inside her. It was like her teenage heart had busted out of its mourning and blossomed back to life in his presence, ignoring the past, the heartache, the brokenness. She mostly played with her dinner. *Poor dinner.* Even Javier's succulent grilled salmon didn't satisfy her. Although the garden strawberries with sweetened sour cream for dessert might have given her one tiny moment of bliss.

It was time to get away from all these feelings. She helped Katie clear a few dishes into the kitchen and, without saying goodbye to anyone, snuck out through the front of the house to check on the construction progress before heading home.

Even in its bare stage of rough framing, the new wing looked amazing to Lily. Part of that she could credit to her construction and fine woodworking crew, but a good part was also due to Miranda's ideas for the space. It wasn't going to be a dusty old study and sitting room with ghosts and rotting horrible memories.

Never again. Instead, Brockman House was going to be completely redefined, beginning with this wing. She climbed the temporary wood stairs and stood where the café would go. From there, she imagined the art gallery lit by the afternoon sun. Liliana closed her eyes, breathing in the beauty of raw wood and dust. Kneeling briefly, she ran her hands along the unfinished fir floors, still warm from the day's sunshine. It was going to be a great thing for Brockman Farms and Graciella and she couldn't have been prouder than if she'd had the idea herself. She was grateful and honored that she'd been given the contract to do the building.

"I thought you'd left," Turner said, jerking her out of her daydreaming.

He leaned against one of the open walls.

It took her a moment to still her racing heart. "What do you want, Turner?"

"I needed a walk. I might ask you the same thing."

"I'm checking the progress here. I came to do it earlier, before Adam dragged me back to dinner." She continued walking around, eying the details of the work, taking mental notes, but her concentration had been blown. All she was aware of were his eyes tracking her.

"Do you often visit random constructions sites to check on things?"

She pinned him with her angry eyes. "When they're my contracts, I do."

"Your contracts?" he asked. He took it all in. *Good, I jolted him out of his lazy stance.* "You work for…" He glanced at the legal paperwork displayed by the door. "Dragonfly Design Construction & Fine Woodworking?"

"I *own* it, Turner. Dragonfly Design is mine."

"You?" Shock transformed his face again. It was sweeter this time since she looked dynamite and wasn't covered in a day's dirt and sweat. Plus, she loved telling people what she did for a living.

"Sexist much?" She might have rolled her eyes, but that would have meant taking her gaze away from his and that seemed an extremely stupid thing to do. One didn't turn one's back on the enemy. "If you don't mind, I have to get home." She walked toward him and the steps, trying to ignore the heat of his concentration.

He put his hand out across the doorway to block her when she tried to pass. Now *he* pinned *her* with a look. One glance was all it had ever taken from him and she faltered. Here in the sweltering evening air, alone with him, it suddenly seemed too much. She looked at his arm. It brushed across her body. A whisper of a touch. A whisper that scattered her pulse in all directions.

"You didn't eat much, Liliana."

"You're in my way," she said. Her stomach had been a bumper car fiasco at dinner. Right now, her voice shook and her mind urged her to get away before she betrayed her feelings for him. *Damn feelings!*

Turner followed her gaze to his arm, then allowed himself a view of her body. A hot current ran through him, tipping all his thoughts of design and construction over into desire. Her touch put him in a trance. Slowly, he lowered his arm. When he looked back at her face, her composure had returned.

Intelligent, charming, efficient, those were all words that had been used to describe Turner's conversation over the years. Dumbstruck had never been one, but right now, he couldn't seem to get his tongue out of his throat.

"Liliana Moreno? Little Lily from when we were kids?"

"Yes, Turner. One and the same."

Hardly. He vaguely remembered her running around with Adam, and he was absolutely certain not one inch of her was the same. No warm-blooded man or woman could forget her. She was the most sensuous creature he'd ever seen.

"You've been gone a while." The words were cold, insulting.

Her tone was a sharp knife across his skin. He knew down to the day exactly how long he'd been gone, how much time he'd...what...lost? It wasn't until dinner that it had hit him that way. Time he'd lost. He'd walked back into a fiction he wasn't part of. Their lives had continued to stream out in one connected story. Unlike his, which suddenly felt stunted, left behind. Strange, that had been his aim, sever all ties. And although he'd told himself he was only coming home for a visit, now — this moment — he didn't like feeling unconnected. *Liliana Moreno making sure to remind me of my faults.*

"You don't like me, do you?" he asked, wishing she'd take one step closer, into him. He could barely remember Lily the girl. Liliana the woman was like nothing he'd ever seen before.

"I don't know you, Turner."

Yet she obviously couldn't stand him. He wanted to know why. He liked her temper, her haughty attitude. It was almost easier to be around than the open acceptance from everyone else. He'd been a selfish bastard for years and she was the only one who called him on it. In an odd way it soothed his guilt. Then there was the feel of her skin, the intoxicating *scent* of her mixed with the heady summer air that made him feel absolute lust for her. He wanted more.

"That dress suits you better than the work clothes you had on this morning." His voice took a step deeper. He gently touched the thin strap of her dress, brushing his fingers across her collarbone. What he wanted to do was taste those sweet lips of hers, stained like rubies from the strawberries she'd silently swooned over at dinner.

She jolted at his touch. Took a step back. "Get out of my way, Turner. I have to get home." Gone was the haughty confidence. For a moment, her eyes lost their fire and turned dark and cold. *Is that fear?*

"Liliana?" he said softly, questioning. Jesus! He was an ass.

He moved out of her path. "I'm sorry, I didn't mean to crowd you, to scare you."

Standing tall, she put her hands on her hips.

"Why are you back, Turner? What are you doing here in my town?"

Her curves might have been generous and warm, but there was no laughter or welcoming tone to her voice. The fire rising from her now was dangerous and strong. She could change in an instant. A chameleon. *More like a dragon. Phenomenal.*

To pay for my sins. To find love. Where the hell had that thought come from? "I don't know." Right this minute he had no idea about anything except wanting to kiss those full lips of hers even if she might poison him. "But…" He smiled as the thought occurred to him. "It's my town too." *What the hell? Since when do I claim this place?* Something happened to him and his emotions around her. He might have been uncomfortable with his admissions except she looked like she was refraining from spitting fire with every word out of his mouth. She was gorgeous. He might as well go with it. Tease the angry goddess now. Fenagle his way out of the situation later. "And this is also my building. Where you're standing."

"Hmmmph," she huffed and shoved past him. "Just because you own something doesn't truly make it yours, Turner."

He took in the view of her walking away. What a view it was. He'd never been a gambling man, but tonight he felt lucky. He decided one last parting shot might be worth it.

"Oh, and, Lily, I guess that also makes me your employer."

She stopped and turned abruptly, her mouth hanging open for one second before she climbed in her truck and slammed the door. Oh yeah, she shot fire. Good thing he was too far away from the flames. She drove out of sight as if a banshee chased her. Turner laughed and all his uncomfortable tension from returning to Graciella melted away. It was, however, replaced by a different kind of tension. A constant humming inside him wondering if Liliana Moreno kissed the way she sparred, full of passion and energy. *All-consuming.*

Chapter Seven

Unable to sleep off his jet lag, Turner knew he needed to *do* something. Jet lag had never bothered him before. He'd always powered through it with work, architectural drawings, client meetings, financial assessments and fixing unexpected problems. He excelled at those things, using work for sustenance the way some used food. At least he hadn't been plagued by nightmares last night. Odd, since this was where they originated.

It was early. The sky streaked with the first pink rays of morning. Five a.m., the clock above the range read. Expecting to be alone, he was surprised when Miranda backed out of the refrigerator and jumped.

"Oh, you scared me." She set eggs, cheese and spinach on the counter. "Morning."

"It's early," he said.

"I'm a morning person. You?"

"Depends," he said. "Is that fresh coffee I smell?"

Her grin reached her eyes and she set coffee mugs in front of him. "I knew I liked you." There was that easy acceptance again. Grabbing the coffee pot, he hid his scowl from her. *You don't even know me.*

"I dropped Cruz at the barns. Do you want to take your coffee and go see him? Or you could stay and have breakfast?"

"I think I'll stay and eat?" He *should* go talk to his brother, but his stomach allowed him to put it off awhile. Besides, he had a feeling he was going to need a good breakfast if he went to the barns. It Cruz wasn't ready to chew him out now, somebody'd probably put him to work.

"Busy day ahead?" he asked.

"Crazy. But I love it. There's such a difference being busy and not loving what you're doing and being passionate for something, don't you think? I never realized how dreadfully dull it was auditing accounts all day, every day for eight, ten, twelve hours. Now I can hardly sleep for how exciting all this is."

His job challenged him, but did he love it? Passion in his career was a foreign concept.

"Would you like me to tell you about the work that's going on? Since it belongs to you. I know you gave Cruz and Adam permission to start construction, but I could share the details."

Initially when he'd heard that T.D. had left him all the farm buildings and a few properties in town, he'd been angry. Now, all his intentions of coming back for a short visit then getting the hell out started to crumble around him. Refueling with great coffee and Miranda's cheerful voice made him curious. If he was honest, it was on a deeper level than from simply a design standpoint. *You still care about this place. You had no idea how much until you set foot back here.*

"You okay?" Miranda asked.

"Sorry. Lost in thought. Hit me."

She smiled. "We're adding a small café, gourmet market and gallery of local art. We've talked about turning the upstairs into a bed and breakfast eventually. And Lily's also renovating the workers' cottages so we can rent them out."

Liliana's face came back into focus. Pretty much since she'd removed her ball cap under the glittering sun on that first morning, she'd been centered in his mind. Somewhere inside him a room had opened up for all the glimpses he'd caught of her since. A showcase of Liliana Moreno's fiery, curious and angry looks. A first for him, making space for a woman. For anyone. When he'd run from here, he'd vowed never to get close to people again.

"Will Dragonfly Design do good work?" Fishing for information, Turner wanted to know more about the company and the owner behind it. He hadn't meant to be a complete jackass last night when talking to her, but damn, he was flipped upside down around her. She seemed able to hold her own against him. Sparring had never been so enlightening.

"Absolutely. Have you not seen any of Lily's work? She's the most talented designer and builder on the west coast. She won't tell you herself, but she's won awards for her work. It's more than construction, Turner. It's art. Her work breathes a life of its own. It's fitting too, don't you think, that the new wing to showcase local artists and chefs is being built by a local?"

"Yes," he said. *Art that breathes a life of its own.* Well, no one had ever said that about his projects. *Nope.* His had been championed for their cutting-edge designs and more importantly the amount of money he brought in with his wealthy clients.

"If you have any input, I'm sure Katie and Lily would appreciate your expertise."

I'm sure Liliana would abhor the idea. He chuckled to himself. "It's great for the farm and the surrounding area," he said. She handed him a bowl full of eggs and a whisk and he put his coffee down and helped her.

"I don't know if anyone besides me will admit it, but we worried what you'd think. I know you gave your consent, but it's different now that you're here."

"You shouldn't have worried." Turner paused for a minute. "This isn't really my home anymore."

She stopped what she was doing and looked at him. "Tell me to butt out if you like, but this place will always be your home if you want it to be."

A week ago, he would have said, "Not in a million years." Today, something made him hesitate. It was too complicated a mess to untangle over jet lag, though. "Brave choice, making an omelet. I never could get them to cook perfectly," Turner said. Much easier to talk about food. Miranda used her spatula to gently coax the eggs away from the sides of the pan.

"Oh, Katie, Turner's joining us for breakfast."

"Lovely," Katie said, and gave his cheek a kiss. "I got carried away out there — seems the tomatoes are ripening early this year with all the heat we've had."

Miranda flipped the omelet and squealed, "It worked!" She divided the delicious-smelling eggs onto three plates and topped each with fresh parsley.

"You're a natural, Miranda." Katie's praise came easily.

"Damn this is good." Turner's surprise made him smile. People always claimed good food could break down defenses. "If this is the stuff you plan on serving in the new café, you ladies will have yourselves a hit."

Miranda and Katie both looked up and stared at him, their smiles spreading.

"Really?"

"You're not just saying that?"

The women spoke at the same time.

"I've been gone awhile, Mom, but my stomach hasn't changed. And it never lies. Miranda, it's a good thing you left the accounting world — Cruz is a lucky man."

Miranda leaned over and kissed his cheek.

"You better hurry and eat, Turner," Katie said. "Javier's on his way and if he doesn't rope you into checking out the updates at the dairy barns, Miranda here will have you wielding a hammer and working on the construction site for the rest of the summer."

I might actually enjoy that. How long had it been since he'd gotten down and dirty with a hammer?

Miranda laughed. "I'm excited for the grand opening and I know Lily has so much work right now and she hasn't been able to spend much time on the theater. I hate for her to have to sacrifice all her employees for the Brockman projects, but she's as ecstatic as we are to see it finished."

"Lily wouldn't have it any other way," Katie said. "She gives over one hundred percent to her projects. It might take longer, but she won't let the theater suffer. Secretly I think she likes working on that project herself. She gets to savor the beautification process."

"I'd like to check out the work that's being done." Turner tried not to sound too enthusiastic at the sound of Lily's name. Damn, he wanted to learn more about her, much more. Plus, cowardly or not right now, anything to postpone another awkward conversation with his brother.

"I'll give you a tour," Miranda said.

"Lead the way, ma'am."

* * * *

"For an accountant, you sure know your way around architectural drawings, blueprints and raw construction," Turner said later when Miranda finished talking and took a breath. She'd described all the aspects of the café, what kind of lighting would be used, the environmentally friendly products they'd sourced, the special placement of the windows. "I'm impressed."

"I follow Lily around like a puppy to soak up her magic."

I'd like to follow Lily around like a puppy.

"My knowledge is shallow, though. So if you ask me too many questions about the design and building, I won't know. Ask me anything you want about the food, the artists and the clientele we hope to attract."

Brockman Farms, the actual house, had always been a hollow, lonely place. No longer, it seemed. Turner had to admit, this project was well thought out. It would create revenue for his family and the local artists, but it would also preserve the nature of the farm. Actually, it would do more than preserve it—it would enhance it.

These women knew what they were doing, his mother, Miranda and Lily. *Liliana.* He liked the way he felt around her, around her construction projects, alive, excited, interested. Hell, he'd even take tongue-tied.

"You really should pick her brains, Turner," Miranda said. "I bet you and Lily have a lot in common. From what Adam's told me, you've designed some amazing structures. Did you have a hand in building them, too?"

Turner walked the length of the café's structure while men worked around him. "Not in a long time," he said.

"There's plenty going on here if you decide you want the physical aspect. Not only here. In town, at the barns, the cottages. Things are changing so much since..."

"Since my father died?" Turner finished for her.

"Yes," Miranda answered quietly. "I think you should talk to Cruz, Turner. He's been waiting. It might do you both a lot of good."

Turner faced her. She was right and she was brave. It was time to talk to Cruz.

"I'm guessing he spends most of the day at the barns?"

She smiled and nodded. "Wait till you see how happy he is in all that mess. I'll see you both later." She waved and headed toward the rose bushes and his mother's garden.

The walk through the lush orchards did nothing to calm his nerves or relax his mind. Any apology or explanation he came up with seemed pathetic.

If *he'd* been brave, he would have kept in touch over the years and he would have come home sooner. But the icy shield he'd built around his heart had turned to fear somewhere, and he'd never known how to thaw it.

He stood at the edge of the fence line by a new barn and watched the cows, breathing in the air that had been a part of his life for so long. Even living in busy urban cities, he'd never been able to completely forget those scents.

"It doesn't ever leave you, does it?" Cruz stood beside him, reading his mind.

Jesus, he needed to pull his emotions together. Turner stayed where he was surveying the land.

"I tried, too," Cruz began.

"Tried?" Turner asked.

"To forget this place. For about a week." Cruz laughed and that right there eased the tension built up in Turner. "I always aimed to return once T.D. was dead."

"Cruz, I—"

"Let me finish." A hint of built-up anger laced his words. "I came back in shock but exhilarated. I wanted to try to make this farm a better place, but it took months to convince me I belonged here and was worthy of finding happiness.

It was a truth Turner wondered about himself. *Do I belong here?* "I owe you an apology, Cruz. You and Adam and Mom. For trying so hard to cut ties. For staying AWOL. For basically being an asshole."

"Dammit, Turner. There's no one to blame here. T.D. is dead. He's the only one responsible for his brutality. I'm no better than you. That's what I'm trying to say. I stayed away too. But the asshole named me executor and I couldn't get out of it. Once I got here, I knew I had to stay. I realized my anger should be directed at T.D., not you. You've come back, Turner. That's all that matters."

"A bit late." Pain and anguish mixed with his guilt and echoed in his words. The workers hustled cows into the barns for their second milking of the day. Sun beat upon the fertile land.

"Late for what, you idiot?"

"To help you," Turner said.

"We need help now. You don't even have to stay — just don't cut us out again."

Through Cruz's words, forgiveness was there, acceptance. Couldn't Cruz see it was different for Turner? T.D.'s blood ran through Turner, not Cruz — somewhere inside there had to be a part of T.D.'s meanness waiting to come out. That was the real reason he'd stayed away and unconnected over the years, because of that threat, that his blood was as cold and ruthless and mean as T.D.'s

"You're nothing like him. You know that. Don't you? None of us are. I don't know how the hell it happened, but the three of us turned out pretty damn good considering."

"You're a fucking mind reader." He wondered if he'd ever feel okay about being T.D. Brockman's favorite son. But knowing his brother saw him as more than that carved out a piece of hope.

"There's a place for you here, Turner, or at least in our lives. It's up to you." Cruz put his hand on his shoulder for a moment.

"Come on. I bet you've forgotten how to milk a cow."

Work would do them both some good. It always had. "I thought they had machines for that nowadays,"

Turner said, his own mood lightened by Cruz's forgiveness and understanding.

"In fact, they do," Cruz shot back. "And you're just in time to help us take apart the rusty old piece of shit and build the new one."

Chapter Eight

Lily hated when her mornings were rushed. *Stupid Turner!* She hadn't gotten in her swim. She'd driven away from her house, forgetting her coffee mug on the roof of her truck. Then she'd muddled, *coffee-less,* through interviews for three new carpenters. She needed a general manager but had shoved that thought in the back of her head, not ready to cede any control over her business yet. Now having skipped breakfast and lunch, she raced into town to spend the last few hours of her evening on the theater. It was all Turner's fault. How dare he invade her sleep, causing her to be both aroused and pissed off? She was sleep-deprived, hungry and discombobulated.

She rolled her window all the way down and tried to soothe her bad mood with the dry, crisp air. She'd studied for a year in Spain, had traveled all over Europe and Asia, vacationed in New Zealand, and still her heart was here in this stunning palate of the Pacific Northwest. She'd never taken it for granted, but the past year had made her even more appreciative and openly acknowledging of this paradise she was surrounded by. The combination of her father's Alzheimer's and him losing the hardware store had tripped Liliana on her joyful, confident path.

Once she'd recovered and charged through her grief, she'd gotten angry and motivated. She'd fixed up an old empty hay barn for her fine millwork and design-construction business, hired employees, got her first contract from a young couple to renovate their hundred-year-old farmhouse, and from there her business had soared. In a small town like Graciella, word of her craftsmanship spread fast. She hadn't looked back yet.

After parking in front of the theater, she walked a few shops down to the Marigold Bakery, another building Dragonfly Design had redone. Over the years someone had drywalled over all the beautiful old brick walls. Uncovered by Lily's crew, those brick walls now reveled in all their glory. The wide planked floors were stained dark and huge new windows graced the front. Liliana took pride in her work, her heart. Ordering her coffee and two chocolate croissants to soothe her grumpy stomach, she calculated how far she could get on the theater floors this week. Hopefully, at the end of today, they would be transformed.

Today she left her headphones in the truck. In the mood for opera, Lily blared her music and started the last round of sanding to the voices that sang through the building and into her blood. Exposed wood and a slight burning scent from the machine permeated the room already stifling with the summer sun.

Even while the work relaxed her, thoughts of Turner snaked in and battered her.

At age seventeen, Liliana had sworn to herself she'd wait forever for Turner Brockman to notice her. Then he'd broken her heart and she'd cursed him to hell and set her mind on another dream—art, design and eventually building or *rebuilding,* as she'd come into her own specialty over the years. Back then, with her heart a mess, she'd sworn never to fall in love with a man again. *Ever.* For a long time, she'd been too busy and dedicated to her studies to even notice any other men. Luckily fate and an internship in Spain had changed all of that. She'd grown up and men had noticed her.

Baco had been her initiation into love. She pictured him walking on the beach in Sant Feliu, the intense cobalt blue of the Mediterranean stretched out before him. Or drinking wine made from his own grapes, his silver hair curling over his ears. Nearly twice her age, he'd been her friend and her lover and he'd taught her so much. And oh, how he'd loved her body. He'd been a safe bet for her, gorgeous, attentive and with no chance of her ever falling in love with him. When she'd left the Mediterranean, she knew they would always be friends.

There'd been a few men since him, casual affairs in the places she'd studied and lived. Casual was key. She'd chosen them when she was ready. And she was always the first to leave. Thinking of them made her smile.

Thinking of Turner made her scowl.

Well, she certainly hadn't waited for him. Finishing her task, Lily tried to put him out of her mind. This project was her peace, her passion. She didn't want him invading any part of it. With a soft cloth, she rubbed the sanded floors, wiping up all the remains of dust. Its smooth surface gave the impression the structure was fragile.

An illusion.

Just like the feel of Turner's hand on her neck. The tips of his fingers certainly alluded to a smoothness, but the pulse beating beneath those fingertips told of strength and hunger. She stopped what she was doing and stepped back, shaken with where her thoughts had traveled, at the tears that burned in her eyes suddenly. How long had she spent forgetting him?

And yet she hadn't, really, not ever.

And now they were both back in Graciella. Part of her had been hopeful that Turner would never return. Another part she kept locked had secretly longed for him to come home, even while her mind warred with her heart over that disastrous notion. Javier spoke of true love, but what good was something as epic as that if it wasn't reciprocated?

The question both her heart and mind currently demanded an answer to was what was his motive for coming home now? She'd always known she'd make her life in the bounty of this land. When she'd asked Turner the other night why he'd returned, he'd said he didn't know. And even though his words had been spoken lightly, he'd had the look of a wild animal caught in a cage, scared and uncertain. Or maybe that was what she wanted to believe she saw, because she couldn't deny the flaming desire in his eyes when he'd looked at her.

How she'd dreamed of that look.

Having it now unsettled her.

As the first coat of stain glided from her sponge to the bare wood floors, darkening them, Liliana thought about desire. She desired him too, or at least her body did. What woman wouldn't? His tall, sharp strength, still boasting that finely tuned athlete's body. The cunning look in his wild green eyes. The rugged, but polished face hardened by simmering emotions he kept below the surface. An idea came to her. *I'll have him. I can take pleasure in a man's body without getting hurt.*

It was almost a sweet relief to think of it that way. Another casual affair. She'd be done with him long before he decided to leave this place again, then she could get him out of her system for good.

* * * *

Only one day's worth of work on the farm and already Turner's body ached. He'd helped the men finish building a few paddocks in the southern pasture. They'd ripped down old stalls in the main barn and several of them had hauled one of the new eight-hundred-pound steel milking machines into place. As if that wasn't enough for one day, they'd started laying down a new roof under the scorching sun.

Over the years, Turner had stayed in great physical shape. He still ran almost every day. He'd been sailing for years and he had boxing bags set up in his apartment in Berlin. But today he was beat. True manual labor like they'd been involved in crushed any exercise routine he'd insisted upon for himself.

But his mind remained restless. They needed more electrical boxes and wire for the updated equipment that was being installed in the old barns and Turner had volunteered to get it. Several of the men were beginning the afternoon milking and Cruz had been on the phone when Turner had left.

He told himself he was just doing them a favor. He'd get in all the favors he could before he left town again. He also told himself he was not going in hopes of seeing Liliana, but if he happened to come upon her, who could be to blame? He even tried to tell himself that he had not been thinking of her all day. *I really am an idiot.*

Working with the men had been good for him, the banter, the easy acceptance, the teasing, the hard labor. But Turner also liked quiet. His mind craved silence and time alone. He'd always been that way — at least since he'd discovered T.D.'s true nature. The memory of running through the orchard with his brothers jarred something else loose. Turner had been loud and funny when he was a kid, outgoing. Competition came naturally to him, that and winning. It wasn't until he'd really understood what an evil man his father was, and that T.D. was in fact grooming Turner to mimic him, that Turner deliberately changed his own nature.

As it turned out, he'd grown to like solitude and quiet. It brought him moments of peace in his life where there hadn't been many. Alone, he could be who he wanted with no one trying to shape him. Alone, he need count only on himself. And alone, he was never responsible for taking care of, or not taking care of anyone.

He pulled up in front of what used to be the old hardware store. *Well*, he thought, getting out of his truck and leaning his face up against the dusty windows to peer inside, *I guess I'm not going to find any wiring equipment here. So much for being helpful.* He took in what used to be a grand, old two-story brick building. The Moreno hardware store. In its day it had stood strong and proud. Now it sagged before him, worn down and embarrassed. And empty, save for some falling-down shelving and lots of dust.

A slight breeze drifted through the small town. A few people strolled by the post office up the street. Cinnamon and sweet sugar mixed with a warm yeasty smell emerged from a bakery. Graciella was still a charming town, with most of the buildings dating back to the late eighteen-hundreds, with a mixture of Spanish Mission and Wild West architecture. The bank remained. It had started as a bank, then evolved into a bank and a saloon until it became more of a saloon and a whore house, and was now a bank again. There was one law office. *I'm surprised there aren't more*, Turner thought wryly. A real estate office drew Turner's attention. It looked freshened up but closed with a sign in the window that read, *Select Graciella Properties for Sale. Please call to make an appointment.* There was a number listed below and the blinds on the windows were drawn.

T.D. had owned a few of these properties. Now they belonged to Turner. It felt odd trying that knowledge on for size. Not horrible, as he'd anticipated. Turner started down the sidewalk, his mind waking up with ideas and questions. A town of interconnected people, needing each other, helping each other—when one thrived, they all did. *Belonging.*

What did that really mean to a man like him who'd cut all ties to this place years ago, and made a point to never be truly connected or *belong* anywhere else, except in the business world? Music intruded into his thoughts and he followed it to the theater. He stood before it, its doors thrown wide open, and wood stain overpowered the fresh air outside.

Drawn by the music, he stepped in. Marilyn Horne singing in *Samson and Delilah*. The deep soprano mixed with the heat and the scents and wrapped their sultry arms around him. And there in the center of it all was Liliana, brushing on a coat of stain, her back to him, the music weeping. She pushed the mop-like brush across the floor in long, fluid strokes completely engrossed in her world. Turner was lightheaded.

The gleaming floor of the intimate theater lobby cascaded in front of her. The place still needed finish work, but Turner could see a difference from when he'd been here a few evenings ago. She wasn't so much changing things as improving, polishing. *A grand restoration or decoration? Both perhaps.* He hadn't been involved in restoration work in years. Usually he was involved in knocking down the old and putting up new, sleek, expensive, modern buildings with price tags to match. Usually he was racing ahead to the next one before the current one was finished.

He wanted to see more, to explore more of what she'd done, but the wet floor wouldn't be happy to have him walk upon it at this moment. Neither would its owner. He tried to step away, but he wasn't fast enough. With a flourish, she brushed the last piece of bare wood, threw her arms open wide and took a step back.

"Ta da!" she exclaimed.

"Gorgeous," Turner said and started clapping. She whipped around at the sound of his voice. From the look of horror on her face, she wasn't as happy to see him as he was her. She started to take a large stride away from him, but Turner grabbed her waist and hauled her to him before she marked up the newly polished floor. He wrapped his arms around her and felt his heavy breathing mirrored by her own, her curves fitting snugly, perfectly against his body.

He wanted to nuzzle his face in her neck, trace the fine skin behind her ear while his arms held on to her warm body. He never wanted to let go.

Chapter Nine

Liliana sucked in her breath and closed her eyes, the feel of him wrapping around her stunning her, leaving her riveted to the spot. His fingers gripped her side and the way he held her as if she was his most precious possession. *Finally,* her heart sang. Her body felt electrocuted.

She had to get away. "Do you mind?" She tried to pry his hands from her.

"Sorry." His voice was muffled against her head. His lips warmed her ear. All she had to do was turn in his arms and she could taste him. Her mind was dizzy.

But he let go. *Good, that's good.* Lily tried to soothe her shaky breaths. She'd almost made a complete fool of herself in broad daylight in the middle of a construction mess. Entertaining thoughts of having an affair with him and actually acting it out in the lobby of the theater were two different things.

"You should be sorry. Damn it, Turner. Quit sneaking up on me. I nearly stepped right onto the floor

I've spent hours perfecting." Liliana inched away from him to the side and walked outside.

"I believe I kept you from falling. Perhaps you owe me a thank-you, Liliana."

He dragged out her name like a lure, slowly pulling her in. She whirled back to face him, her mouth open in shock. Narrowing her eyes, she shot imaginary arrows at him. *Is he grinning? God, he has a sexy grin.*

"Here, I'll help you." He took a step closer. She took one back. She was against the door with nowhere else to go.

Why is he staring at me like that? He wasn't grinning now. She could hardly breathe, and she couldn't read the language on his face. First there was that cocky attitude of his, then this other silent language he spoke that she couldn't understand, but felt in her blood, a whisper that only she could hear. Maybe if she touched his face, then she could read the words. Before she could reach up, he spoke. *Haughtiness back in full force.*

"It's like this, Liliana, 'Thank you for saving me, Turner.'" Gone was the sensual world he'd almost let her into. "Now you try." He actually had a twinkle in his eye. He was laughing at her!

"Go to hell!" She shoved him out of the way and took off outside, mumbling, "Who does he think he is? *'Thank you for saving me.'* Hah! I don't need anyone to save me. Not ever again. Shit!" She sagged against the very locked door of her truck.

"Need help?" he asked, casually leaning against the theater opening, aiming his smirk right at her.

"No, I do not need help, not from you, not from anyone. What I need is for you to leave me alone so I can close up and get to my next project."

Turner's smirk slid into a full smile, not sexy this time. More worthy of a jaguar ready to pounce. "It looks to me like you locked yourself out."

"I did not." She stalked back past him into the lobby. *Go away,* she pleaded silently. Liliana stopped at the edge of the wet floor. "Shit! Shit! Shit" she said again.

"Such a lovely mouth on such a beautiful woman," Turner said, laughing at her.

"Again, with the sexism. You're hardly original, Turner. Can't you go away?" Hands on her hips, she confronted him.

"Not until I know you've found your keys. And I meant it." He leaned in and his voice had grown deeper. All of him focused on her lips. "You have a lovely mouth."

If my legs give out, will he save me? Or will I be your prey, caught?

"Where are they?"

Where are what? She stood at the edge of the floor. He stood below her on the steps. There wasn't anywhere to go unless she planned on walking across the wet floor. Her keys were inside. Inside where she couldn't get to them until the stain had dried. At least twelve hours from now.

"Come on. I'll give you a ride," he said, back to his cocky casual self.

Is he pleased I left my keys inside where I can't reach them? Liliana stood, reeling on an emotional rollercoaster. She could walk home, she told herself. It was a small town, but then there was the teeny hill she lived on, at the top. Most wouldn't necessarily call it teeny. It could take her two hours on foot. Hours she couldn't afford to waste. Hours she needed to spend catching up on her bookkeeping. Honestly, she wasn't sure her shaky legs could carry her a block.

"Fine, but I'll pay you." She closed the doors to the theater, hoping no one would get a stupid idea and try to sneak in overnight.

"Pay me?" Turner laughed, a loud, full-bodied sound that nearly had her joining in, except for the fact that he was making fun of her and she felt suddenly fifteen again and small.

"Yes, Turner, as in money. I don't take charity."

"Charity?"

"Quit laughing at me," she said, shooting him daggers with her eyes. She brushed past him.

"I'm not making fun. You're being absurd, Lily — "

"Don't call me absurd." She laced her words with an edge of fire.

"This isn't charity. It's what friends do, help each other."

"Friends?" She couldn't help her tone of disgust. Turner opened the door for her and closed it after she stepped into the truck.

"Okay, neighbors then."

"Neighbors?" Her temper spilled over. "Neighbors, in case you need a refresher course, are people who live in the same neighborhood. Who see one another daily. Who take care of one another. Neighbors are not immature boys who run away from their loved ones and responsibility and stay away for almost twelve years."

She noticed his flinch, like he'd been sucker punched. *Oh, shit!* She had not meant to spew her childhood hurt all over him.

Immediately, she sensed a change in him. He gripped the steering wheel, his knuckles holding his anger. Gone was the mocking grin and the light in his eyes, the casual stance of his body. Everything about him tensed up. Even the air around her felt heavy.

"Fine," Turner began, his words like ice on her skin. "Pretend I'm a cab driver. Which way, ma'am?"

Each word was a blade, sharp, cutting. He didn't look at her but kept his gaze straight ahead.

All the frustration and anger seeped out of her. "I'm sorry, Turner. Your life is none of my business."

Silence greeted her.

"Turner?"

"I said, which way?"

She turned and looked out of her window. *Good job, Liliana, now he's pissed at you and he has every right to be.* She'd taken her emotions out on him and he didn't deserve it. She liked it better when she could be angry at him. "Left out of town up Maple Hill. You remember the cliffs?"

Liliana let her window down and was met with the scents of the dry amaranth and barley fields. The afternoon heat baked everything. Silence sat between them like dirt baked in the desert sun. Normally she liked quiet, but not this kind. "Turner, I am sorry. I have no right to judge you. I get snippy when I forget to eat. Oh!" She reached into her shirt pocket, pulled out the candy bar she'd forgotten about and ripped it open. *Mmm, sugar, peanuts, chocolate.*

"You were right."

"What?" That was the last thing she expected him to say.

"Can we drop it? It's not something I'm proud of."

"I'm sure you had your reasons." Reasons, which as much as she wanted to know were none of her business. "Really I didn't mean—"

"You like opera?" Turner changed the subject.

She stared at him for a moment. His knuckles were no longer rigid, but he still held himself separate. "I love it," she answered, unsteady with this other side of him. Perhaps it was for the better, however, to keep things light and casual between them. Easier to walk away once they were finished with each other. She concentrated on the caramel layer of goodness and put the empty wrapper back in her pocket.

"I saw Marilyn Horne in *Samson and Dalila* in Monte Carlo when I was twenty. It was the first time I fell in love."

"*You* like opera?" Who was this man next to her?

"And you think I'm sexist." He shot her a quick glance and raised his left eyebrow. "Love, Liliana. Not just like. You know I'm getting quite used to that haughty sneer you keep giving me. Makes your mouth look lovely *and* dangerous."

She snapped her mouth shut and turned forward again, blush rising in her cheeks.

"Which drive is yours?" They'd climbed the hill that led to a few secluded houses on the cliffs.

"The last one. It's new, full of gravel. You can't miss it." He turned slowly down her long driveway. Her cottage was still invisible through the overhang of tree branches, and some maples were twisted in with the evergreens. The type of peace she loved greeted them. The water, deep below the cliffs, was calm this evening. Even the heat hovered around them in a lazy afternoon nap under a blanket of towering fir trees. Once he'd parked, she glanced over at his silence. He stared, wide-eyed. Barely visible was a small nod he gave. Of approval, acceptance? She couldn't tell. For some uncomfortable reason, Liliana desperately wanted to know. There was no way in hell she was going to ask him.

"It's yours, isn't it?"

"Yes, Turner. I do know my own house. Did you think I would have led you down the wrong driveway?"

"I mean, you built it, didn't you?"

"Oh." She leaned back. "Yes. How did you know?"

Before them, in a small opening of trees, where the land had been cleared, sat Lily's home, her love. Built in the Old Spanish Mission style, it wasn't big, but it exuded her spirit. Plastered in a soft red pomegranate, with mustard trim curving around the arched windows and gables. Dark clay tiles fanned over the roof and a dusty brick pathway led the way into the house. Lush plant life surrounded them. Bougainvillea ran down the southern façade of the house, and glazed planters sat overflowing with flowers.

"It's gorgeous, Lily." Turner's voice was low, hushed. "Seductive."

Suddenly Lily wished she hadn't rolled her window up yet. She was very much aware now of how little space sat between them. Mixed with the heat of the car was Turner's scent, the sweat and strength coming off his body. It surrounded her. *He likes my design, my home.*

"It's brilliant."

"What?" she asked, her system still in shock.

He got out of the car and walked a few paces in front of her house. She stalked after him trying like crazy to shush the music in her heart. "You think it's brilliant?" She had no idea until he'd spoken how much she secretly wanted him to like her home.

"Can I see the rest?"

If she let him inside, she might never let him leave. But he would eventually, that she was sure of. This was getting more dangerous by the minute. *He's asking about the house, not your body or your heart, Lily, get a grip.* But her house *was* her heart.

"Lily?"

Turner cocked his head and stared at her. The light was back in his powerful eyes, but this time there was no hint of teasing. They were open, wanting, hungry. And all of that directed at her. If she believed in magic, she might believe he could see into her deepest desires. To the ones that thrilled as much as frightened her. "Are you all right? You look like you're about to faint or…"

"Turner… You… I…" He stalked her. Their eyes locked together. He didn't stop, but lifted her and bound their lips together.

Holy mother of…! Fireworks streaked through her. Her head tilted back in invitation for him to ravage her mouth. A fierce energy hummed in her body, brought to life by him, by them together. She melted, was on fire. Starving, she'd never been this hungry in her life. How had she survived without this power? With equal force, she kissed him back, diving into him. *Oh, my God*, the things his mouth stirred in her core. In one move, she lifted her legs around his waist and struggled to get her arms out of his grip so she could touch him. She'd waited so long to touch him.

The summer heat engulfed them. The soft breeze tantalized. Turner knelt in the grass with her. He was her sunshine, tuning her body, her senses into *everything*. The warm surface of the ground welcomed her and blades of grass tickled along her neck. Dried summer dirt and sweet pea perfume invaded her. The deep inner rumbling of the earth seeped into her. And Turner was all hot, hard, soft lips, hands digging into her skin. Their bodies pressed together as she absorbed him, trying to find that beautiful friction everywhere. Alive, she'd never felt so dynamic, so aware.

They were like wild animals rolling over each other, neither one coming up for air. Lily tore his shirt up from his waistband where she could finally touch his skin, soft and hard and so warm. In one motion, he opened her shirt and found her body beneath and the lacy curve of her black bra. When he kissed her there, his lips sent a shiver straight down her spine. She arched into that feeling. *More.*

Had she known it would feel like this, taste like this, be so absolutely potent, consuming her in one breath? Her core felt vulnerable, exposed. As though she were leaning out of an open airplane, ready to jump. No fear, only a lightness on every inch of her being.

I am yours, Turner. Unbidden, the thought soared through her, her most secret desire, her truth.

No, no, no! Panic swooped in and choked that light away from her. She pulled away from the kiss. *There will be no exposing my heart to him.* She would not lose herself to him again. She belonged to no one but herself.

Control, she needed to be in control when and if they ever made love. And this wild frenzy would leave her in a pile of ashes. Lily covered her face with her hands and willed her body to disappear before Turner caught a glimpse of her secret emotions.

Chapter Ten

"Lily?" His breathing was heavy. Sunlight bounced off the car, lit their faces. The glare shocked him back to earth. He traced the soft skin of her cheek. Even their shadows caressed. The raw vulnerability of the moment struck him like a healing over of some ancient scar. "Look at me, Liliana." But when she did, he wished he hadn't asked.

It wasn't fear or confusion he saw. She was downright pissed. The full force of her grenade powered toward him. He might have started it with that kiss but if she hadn't grabbed onto him and kissed him back like he was her next breath, if he hadn't been absolutely certain she wanted him, in that moment he would have pulled away. "Don't glare at me. You wanted that to happen too." He rolled away and sat up.

"Oh, now you know me so well, Turner Brockman. You think I make out with random men on my front lawn every day." She struggled to button her shirt.

He stared at her. She'd tried to hide it, but he heard the tremble in her voice that matched her shaking fingers. She was afraid, of him, of herself? He couldn't tell, but he was determined to find out why.

"No, Lily. I don't think that, not even close. Don't put words in my mouth. It doesn't suit you. We kissed each other." He gestured between them. "It's called getting carried away. The sparks have been there since I came back. Intense sparks, I might add."

He offered a hand to help her up, which she smacked away before standing on her own and starting toward the house.

Maybe she had a right to be annoyed that they'd almost made love on her front lawn, but they were both to blame. He might be a jerk for having stayed away from his family for years, but what had just happened here belonged to both of them and he didn't appreciate being brushed off like an inconsiderate asshole.

"Be pissed at me if it makes you feel better. You've perfected that. Add whatever wound I've inflicted on you this time to my list of transgressions. But that was the most explosive, amazing kiss I've ever had. I have never felt *anything* close to that in my life. I think you're angry at yourself for enjoying it. For feeling that incredible energy zap through us."

She stopped, abruptly, but did not turn around. *Wonder what battle she's fighting now? The one inside her that knows I'm right? Or the one that wants to put her fist in my eye?* Too bad he couldn't see her face. Annoyed as he was at her, he'd have loved to watch the storm roll across her features.

"What time do you want me to pick you up in the morning?" Turner asked, his voice low, heated.

"What are you talking about?" She whipped around. There was that fiery glare.

Huh? It didn't, as he'd anticipated, burn him to the ground. In fact, he liked matching her emotions. Holding his own had never felt so fantastic. Their fires were drawn to each other. No, hers woke his up, encouraged him to *feel*. It shattered all the fears inside him. *This is where I belong.*

He steadied himself. Tucked that thought away for later. "Seems to me you'll need a ride to work."

"I'll find a ride. Thank you very much."

"Why, when your personal taxi is at your service?" He made a mocking bow in front of her and stood, meeting her glare with one of his own. "I'm giving you a ride, Lily. What time?"

"Fine. Be here at six-thirty, sharp."

"Oh, and Lily." Turner climbed into his truck and rolled his window down. Shooting her a wicked grin he said, "Don't worry, we'll have another chance."

"Another chance at what?" she asked.

"At making love." Before her outrage could blast him to pieces, he pushed on the accelerator and turned down her driveway. This time, he was the one leaving her fuming in the dust. It wasn't quite as satisfying as he'd imagined, with the taste of her sugary lips lingering on his. Because all he wanted to do was turn around and beg her for more.

She should have argued with him about the ride, about making love. She should beat it into his head that she did not need him. In any way. But she honestly didn't have the strength. She was exhausted and hungry, and her emotions were strung out in so many directions that she knew she'd lose much more than the argument.

"Damn! Damn! Damn!" Liliana stalked through her house. She made her way to the back, stripping off each piece of clothing, not bothering to pick them up. Sitting on the back steps long enough to remove her boots, she then dove right into the clear blue water of her pool. Only after the water surrounded her did she let the tears come. She swam two lengths underwater without coming up for a breath, begging the pressure on her lungs to banish her unsteady emotions.

Slowly the smooth caress of the cold water calmed her anger, her annoyance, even her tears, but it did nothing to still the overwhelming beating of her heart. Floating on her back, her eyes closed, Lily allowed herself a few moments to think about that kiss. So much more than a kiss. Primal and electrifying and amazing. He was a match striking her on fire. She could still taste him and her body hummed with need. And all of it was nothing compared to his words. *'Most explosive, amazing kiss...I have never felt anything close to that.'* Her heart nearly burst open right then and there and screamed, "I'm yours!"

Could she really have a casual affair with Turner Brockman then toss him aside? Maybe Javier was right. Maybe she was still in love. Dammit! How could she be after all these years? She'd grown up. She'd had passionate affairs. And she knew how to walk away.

But no kiss, no embrace had ever blasted open her heart like that.

And her heart wanted everything.

The sun began its descent and Lily shivered. Swimming to the side, she dried off, dressed in oversized sweats and pulled out the gazpacho from the fridge. With leftover garlic bread, she sat out back to feed her empty stomach with sharp flavors. Evening light played upon the pool's surface. Cold tomato-cucumber soup, garlic and wine filled her senses. She ate like a scavenger

"Too bad you can't fill my heart too," Liliana said to the bowl of soup.

Her heart, her passion, her life. All three were twined together. *So much at stake.*

Lily had waited a lifetime for that kiss, and now that she'd tasted Turner Brockman, now that she'd felt his desire for her, she was more scared than she'd ever been of anything in her life. It had gotten out of control so fast she couldn't clearly remember it all. One minute he'd singed her with a hot, carnal branding and the next they were rolling around on the ground ready to devour each other. She felt them light each other up. Was that what he meant when he'd said, *'For feeling that incredible energy zap through us'*? Had he felt that full-of-life desperate need too?

Turner was right when he'd said she wanted it. She did, but how could it possibly be more than that when she didn't even like him? In order to like someone, you had to know them. And she didn't know a thing about Turner Brockman anymore except that he'd been chasing money around the globe for twelve years without a single thought to his family. At least, that's what she told herself to stem the feelings she had for him.

And how dare he assume there'd be another chance! Liliana furiously loaded the dishwasher. If there another chance, she would have to be the one in control because she knew how easy want could spill over into need. And she couldn't allow herself to need Turner

Brockman then watch him walk away from Graciella again. If that kiss was any indication, this time it would break her.

Chapter Eleven

Her temper had not simmered down by morning. Another night tossing and turning left plenty of room for being furious at Turner. Determined to knock that cocky grin off his face, she waited outside. But when he pulled up and pushed the door open for her from the driver's seat, he wasn't grinning at all. Instead it was like he could see right through her with laser-focused eyes. Eyes that nearly had her running back inside. But she'd be damned if she'd let him see her cowardice. It was the amount of work she had to finish today that finally had her walking toward him. She climbed into the truck in silence with a scowl on her face and it stayed that way almost until they arrived at the theater.

Without taking his eyes from the road, he placed a pink bakery bag on her lap and the smell of glorious fresh cinnamon morning buns overwhelmed her. By some miracle, other than gifting her breakfast, he left her alone in peace. She wasn't sure how she felt about that. It didn't lessen any of her nerves. Instead she ate and tried not to let him hear her sigh of rapture at the warm pastry.

After he parked, Turner finally spoke, "What happened to the hardware store? I thought your father owned that too?"

Liliana had her hand on the door. She'd expected him to be a jerk this morning with a smug look on his face, but he kept surprising her. She turned in the direction Turner was staring. The empty building that now boasted neglect, dirt and a suspiciously generic *Premier Real Estate, No Trespassing* sign. It was a damn thorn in her side every day to see it and still not have any answers to her questions about who now owned it and what they planned on doing with it.

"I don't know." She glanced back at Turner, uncertain how much to tell him, then back at the building. "Papá sold it to T.D. when I was abroad almost a year and a half ago now." There was no way in hell her father had been in his right mind when that transaction had gone down. It made her so furious she wanted to break something. "When I came back and started asking questions, all I got were closed doors. After…" She glanced at him. "Since your father's death, Cruz has been trying to organize all his paperwork. Figure out which properties T.D. actually owned, if he had a partner or sold any of them, because none of the deeds were filed. When we call the Premier number, we get a machine. No one's called back. It's weird. From the beginning I've had this feeling that the whole deal was done illegally. Miranda called her contacts at the IRS and apparently this Premier Real Estate is a real business, but that's all we know for sure. Even the title company can't 'find' any of the transfer papers. They think we're all losing it."

He tilted his head in confusion.

He didn't believe her. "Jesus, Turner don't look at me like that." Was she merely an emotional woman who couldn't take care of herself, in his eyes? Why would she think age had matured him, given him any depth? "I get gut feelings all the time and I'm usually right. You can think it's all nonsense. I don't care. You're the one who asked." With a huff, she got out of the truck and slammed the door. Good Lord, it felt like all she did around this infuriating man was slam doors.

He caught up to her in front of the theater. "I wasn't making fun, Lily," he said, taking her arm lightly. She shook him off.

"Your look said it all," she said.

"My look was one of confusion, not disbelief. I *have* been gone a long time, Lily. I'm trying to understand everything."

She didn't know whether to believe him or not. "I don't have time for this right now. Thanks for the lift."

"You have a unique way of thanking people, Liliana."

His voice deepened, a purr over her skin. The purr of a lion before a kill. He teased and mocked her, and she was all but a puddle at his feet because of the sound of his voice. Liliana closed her eyes and tried to pull up some of her papá's patience. When she opened them again, he'd moved a fraction closer, his eyes searching hers. How was a woman supposed to have any patience around his hot gorgeousness, even if he was a jerk? It was a struggle to calm her words, but she'd do it. She wouldn't be accused of being immature, of letting her emotions rule her world. Just because they did, didn't mean she'd let him gloat. "Thank you, Turner Brockman. I appreciate the ride. Now if you'll excuse me, I need to get my keys so I can visit my job sites. *I* have a business to run."

"No problem." He flashed a casual grin and turned to walk away. He wasn't sure which he liked better, the passionate nature of her temper, her emotions spilling out, or this attempt to control them. He could have told her it didn't work, that even though her words had taken on a smooth, mocking kindness, her emotions burned bright in her gorgeous brown eyes. *Probably waiting for the right time to singe me.* It was as though she'd been stoking the coals overnight, ready to destroy him when they shot into flame. *Go for it. Have your way with me. I'm already lost in your fire.* The thought should have stunned him, but ever since last night when one kiss from her had had his life settling into place, he wasn't shocked. He was intrigued and awake and felt pieces of his heart being stitched back together. He also wanted to kiss that sexy mouth of hers again.

Another unfashionable outfit of work clothes graced her body. But all he could see was the lacy black bra she'd worn underneath yesterday. She'd tucked her hair under her hat again, like the first day they'd met. Like she was torturing him on purpose, hiding her beauty. God, he'd only just seen her for the first time a few days ago and yet she'd invaded his entire being. Her scent, sawdust and sweet flowers, emanating from her skin. Eyes like dark amber lit in a flame. Her mouth, equally alluring whether it was snapping at him or kissing him. Mmm, he kept coming back to those lips. He thought he might die if he didn't get to taste that mouth again soon, but he wasn't ready to incinerate yet. Besides, he enjoyed unbalancing her. It made him feel marginally better about his own desires and feelings floundering inside him.

Moving toward his truck, he glanced back and watched her unleash her temper on the theater doors, hauling them open and muttering up a storm.

What the hell. Let's see how it feels to get singed.

"One more thing."

"What, Turner?" she said in exasperation.

Turner leaned in and kissed her softly once on the lips, lingering for too many seconds to count. Too few for his liking. He didn't know whether he should pat himself on the back for the willpower to pull away after one or kick his own butt. Cinnamon morning buns were now his favorite food, ever. The shock running through her made him smile and he finally climbed into his truck. "Have a good day, Lily. I'll see you later." He watched her stomp inside before he pulled out of town. On his way, he memorized the phone number on the window of the real estate office. Turner had an uncomfortable feeling about Premier Real Estate too.

* * * *

Why would a real estate office, the *only* one, in a secluded, beautiful coastal town — that was being given a new life — have their blinds closed, the doors locked and a phone number leading directly to an answering machine? Turner replaced the receiver in its cradle after calling for the fourth time in days.

And not one afternoon, or one day, but constantly, from what Turner had seen and gathered from his questions. It wasn't what he would call good business, especially for a realtor who stood to make a chunk of change from the deals to come. An intelligent realtor would have their doors open, their blinds up, flowers in the window boxes, a welcome sign. Hell, they might go door to door to the other local businesses, greeting people firsthand.

Turner finished his run and headed to the dairy barns to find Cruz. The morning had started out with a fine mist in the air morphing the land into a foggy blur and as fog had a way of doing—something else he'd always loved—muffling the noises around him. As the sun rose, much of it dissipated, but as he strode through the orchards, patches of white still greeted him. Ghosts teasing in and out. A rare scent seeped into him, the morning's leftover dew, so heavy he could almost taste its damp seduction mixed with patches of dirt, lush trees and even rotting blossoms under his feet being warmed by the sun. It slammed into him with memories.

He'd walked this path many times in his teens. A teenager who'd gone from the golden boy to a changed person overnight. A boy who'd finally quit believing there would ever be a shred of goodness in T.D. Turner had cursed the fact that he had so little control over the man's bitter actions. He'd let the shame in loving T.D. for so long wash over him. He'd paced the rows of apple trees, looking for escape. For a way to beat his old man, and finally for silence. Because, for so many years, Turner had been naïve. He'd been happy and carefree and hopeful that there was good in everyone, even his father. He'd been a fool for believing so long, for hoping.

Trying to outmaneuver T.D., to fend off the beatings he'd unleashed upon Turner's brothers was hard enough. The knife to the heart had come in realizing T.D. had wanted Turner to emulate him, the mean, manipulative and feared patriarch. Turner had snapped when he'd choked down that realization.

T.D. had surprised Turner for his eighteenth birthday by buying him a whore with a birthday card that said *It's about time you got laid, son.* A gift from his father? It had made him sick to his stomach. He'd run, choking back his vomit. It had been Turner's senior year in the middle of September and the next week he'd quit the football team, quit everything, all the sports he loved and was good at. Anything that gave T.D. cause to be proud of Turner, Turner had trashed. He didn't want T.D.'s pride in him. He didn't want any connection at all to T.D.

Once he'd graduated, he'd left. Only he couldn't get far enough. He could never get far enough.

Now he was back on this sacred land as the fog melted away from the earth, back to the sun. In the past that memory had always choked him. But he felt different being here now. Safe, alive, perhaps the gift of a new beginning? He was still unsure how to reconcile the fact that this place linked him to T.D.

Was there more for him here than a tainted connection to a past he didn't want to own? He'd once loved the land, but, he had to admit, he wasn't interested in the farming life like his brothers were. What was he interested in? He stared at the barn that was already bustling with activity at seven in the morning. The workers moved in sync. Adam and several men were finishing the last paddock closest to the barns. Cruz was climbing down from the roof of the new employee housing a few yards away. Building things. His brothers were putting this place back together, making a community again, something to be proud of.

Build things. The phrase cracked another part of him open. He loved to build things and if he looked back, that was what he'd always loved. Even in college he'd done construction work over the summers to pay for his tuition. Even with his mind set on bigger and better things, he'd loved the physical hands-on connection of building beautiful structures. Soon after graduation, he'd been seduced by the rocket-speed movement of his career. Lulled by the sleek, wealthy companies that hired him to design fancy buildings all over the world. Seduced by the control that was placed in his hands. He actually loved designing new structures too. He'd just gotten so far from the connection he felt to all of it.

Connection, community, a place for him here? Could he belong in Graciella, not just existing, but doing something he loved? All around him the town was changing. It was time for him to step up to the plate, to understand exactly what T.D. had left him. More importantly, to figure out what he intended to do with his inheritance in this place that was both his nightmares and his salvation.

Turner stepped into the barn office and grabbed water bottles out of the cooler. First, he headed in Adam's direction. "Hey, little brother, got a minute?"

"You look way too clean to be out here," Adam teased, his face covered in sweat and a smile.

Adam looked relaxed, if that were possible, hoisting planks of wood. Relaxed or not, his reflexes were still top notch, Turner noticed with a grin when Adam caught the bottle Turner pitched at him. "I'm going to grab Cruz."

"Something up?" Cruz plucked a bottle from Turner's hands and downed the water in one gulp.

"I've been meaning to ask, what's the deal with Premier Real Estate?"

"Ahh," Cruz grinned. "The prodigal son finally interested in seeing what T.D. left him?"

"Isn't there some sort of initiation back into the fold for this yahoo?" Adam said. "Horse trough dunking? Manure collecting? Ripping off old roof tiles."

"You two are hilarious," Turner said. Then, before he let go any longer, "I'm sorry I was absent for the last decade."

"Don't you mean, 'Sorry for being an insufferable asshole'?" Adam joked.

"I've been that much of a shithead, huh?"

Adam's smile faded. "We missed you, idiot." Turner saw no malice. Only longing. Fuck, he'd missed his brothers too.

"Yeah, me too." His brothers smiled. Forgiveness, acceptance. He was grateful for it.

Gesturing them into the office, Cruz sat down on the desk and rubbed his neck with his hand. "T.D. left us a shitshow."

"Premier appeared immediately after T.D.'s death," Adam said.

"Appeared?" Turner asked, leaning against the wall.

"As you know, T.D. had been hovering over any downtown property that seemed ready to go up for sale or where an owner might have fallen on hard times." Cruz pulled open one of the file drawers and eased out two overflowing expanding files of paperwork. He tossed them on the desk for Turner.

"We still don't know the details of each one he actually purchased or sold. His will listed three, but his will dates months before his death. It's been hell trying to settle everything because of the layers of lies and secrecy. Jake's been working overtime, but even with the audit finished, things have dragged. Unfortunately, there are a few secrets we're still uncovering. We suspect he may have had a partner. One we can't locate."

"After his death," Adam began, "the signs in all the vacant buildings that held generic For Lease and No Trespassing signs were replaced by Premier signs."

"Like the Morenos' hardware store," Turner said.

"Exactly. That's another reason we want thing settled. It affects other people."

"Lily said she came to you for help. Why was she and not her father asking you?" Turner said. "And why did she wait until after the deal to become suspicious? Hell, why did Mr. Moreno sell it in the first place?"

Silence met Turner. "I think you're going to be playing catch-up around here," Adam said. "Mr. Moreno has Alzheimer's. He was only diagnosed a year ago. None of us knew about it until Lily returned. They think he'd been deteriorating for years, but he lived alone, and Lily was traveling for her education."

"Christ," Turner swore.

"Exactly," Cruz continued. "The store was in financial trouble. T.D., or his partner, swooped in and the deal went through. But Lily believes her father never signed anything himself."

"And the deeds are mysteriously missing or lost?" Turner said. "Or stupidly haven't been filed yet?"

Cruz nodded. "I called Premier and spoke with a woman named Elizabeth Wells. She was very nice. The kind of nice that makes you sick to your stomach, a woman playing dumb, only you can hear the cat hissing under her pretend naïve answers. I think she was T.D.'s real estate agent, among other things. She may be the partner we're looking for."

"What did all these women see in him?" Turner said, disgusted.

"It must have been his charm," Adam deadpanned. For a second silence greeted the men then Turner howled with laughter. Cruz was next, doubled over at the desk, nearly choking on his water. Adam grinned.

"God," Turner began when he could catch his breath. "It sure feels good to laugh at the bastard."

"Anyway," Cruz continued, "when I mentioned I had questions concerning the properties she handled with T.D, she was all candy until I mentioned the Morenos' store. I could almost hear the claws come out. We set a time to meet and she didn't show up. That was a few weeks ago, before you came home. I haven't followed up because things have been crazy. And I've been trying do what I can to help with the wedding."

Turner couldn't get over how excited and happy Cruz was. "Still can't believe you're getting married. If I remember correctly, you swore you were never falling into that trap," Turner teased him.

"He's lucky she wants to marry him." Adam smacked Cruz on the shoulder.

"True," Turner said. Standing here in the early morning, joking with his brothers, was something he'd never imagined when he came home intent on burying ghosts.

"Speaking of weddings." Cruz stood. "The three of us, Jake and Miguel have an appointment this afternoon at the house for tuxedo fittings. Miranda hired a tailor."

"I don't know if the people at the wedding will be able to handle this enormous amount of good looks in one place," Adam said with an exaggerated sigh.

The three brothers looked at each other, at their dirty farm clothes, boots and shoes full of mud over their sweat-covered bodies and started laughing all over again.

Chapter Twelve

Now that he no longer saw what T.D. had left him as a burden, Turner was eager to help solve the property mystery. Maybe Cruz and Liliana had been ignored because the person on the other end knew who they were and what they represented. He, on the other hand, had a different card to play, a card guaranteeing him a response.

"Hello, I'm with Klein Worldwide Development Strategies. I'm interested in speaking to someone from your agency about the buildings for sale in Graciella, Oregon." Turner left a quick message with his international cell phone number.

Lily had a bad feeling that things were fishy concerning her father's property, and he didn't discount her senses at all. Instincts had gotten him far in his career. Anyone who'd ever had a taste of the real estate business or development knew emotions raged. Drama was high. Scandals were plentiful.

And now his gut told him whatever was going on with Premier was bigger than one hardware store. He might have been gone for twelve years, but he wasn't blind. In a word, Graciella was paradise. A natural beauty with her dark blue waters that remained some of the cleanest in the country. Emerald-green rolling grasslands intermixed with crops and orchards and evergreen trees. To the east, watching over it all were aged mountains. Crops grew well, new vineyards blanketed the low valley near the coast, and rarely a day passed without the scent of the sea in the crisp air.

Additionally, to many around the world, this town was still unknown, nestled into its own Brigadoon. Untouched, but not for long. Change could be good, but it could also leave a town vulnerable to predators who didn't care a thing for preserving any natural beauty or charm, predators with dollar signs in their eyes and their hearts.

Paradise it was, indeed. Just what kind of paradise it would *become* and under whose keen eye were apparently to be determined.

It was after seven when the men had finished with the tailors. Turner was the last to be fitted. Adam had taken off for his house, Miguel to his family and Cruz had gone in search of Miranda. When Turner made it downstairs, Katie had left pasta salad and cold fried chicken in the fridge for dinner. Damn, she still made the best fried chicken he'd ever tasted.

Miranda and Cruz were standing in the garden with their arms around each other. She was laughing at something he said. An intimate space surrounded them and Turner felt as though he was intruding.

Eating dinner by himself while watching them together through the window didn't have much appeal so he piled some pasta and a couple more pieces of chicken into a bowl, grabbed a beer and headed out front. He found himself drawn again to Lily, to her work. She'd invaded his entire body. A spell had been cast to bring him near her or whatever she touched. The wing now had walls and a roof, but no windows. Her crew was good. They made quick progress, but they took great care with their work too. He sat down on the steps and looked at the land before him, the slope down to the narrow road leading up to the Brockman House lined by trees and patches of crops sneaking their way in-between. From where he sat, he could see all the way downtown into the valley below.

And that was where he was sitting when Lily drove up. As if he'd gone there knowing she was about to appear, or him arriving had lured her to him. Just who had cast the spell upon whom wasn't crystal clear. There was a pull between them. It was a connection he longed for. One he was nearly desperate to explore. Every time he was near her, it intensified.

God, she's a beautiful mess. Curls snuck out from under her hat. Plain work clothes looked as if they hadn't been washed in days. Dust and a bit of wood stain splattered across her cheek. A warrior prepared for battle. She was breathtaking.

"Finally made it to this job site? Seems like a pretty important one to leave hanging till the end of the day." He loved provoking her.

"This is the second time I've been here today. And I always check Brockman House at the end of the day regardless of whether I've been here helping or working on my other sites, Turner. Don't even think of micromanaging this project."

"I wouldn't dream of it." *I wouldn't mind micromanaging your body.*

"Did you get banished from the kitchen?" Liliana asked, her voice in that huff he loved. She practically pummeled the truck door shut and walked to him. He wondered if she always slammed doors as though she was smacking sense into someone, or if he was the only one who brought out that side of her.

A grin broke out across his face. "Good evening to you too."

"Oh, don't give me that good-evening bullshit with that snobby air of yours." She stopped on the steps beside him. "Hungry? Looks like you've got enough there for an army." She pierced him with a scowl, just as her stomach made an obnoxious, embarrassing low growl.

He could have heard it in Berlin. He laughed and, before she could stalk off, pulled her down beside him. "Apparently I'm not the only one who's hungry." He put the bowl in her lap, stole a quick kiss from her warm lips and took immense pleasure in the tempest shooting through her eyes. "Eat. I'll be right back."

What the hell was he doing here, again? It was bad enough she hadn't been able to get him out of her mind all day. Every day, since he'd been here. Bad enough that while daydreaming of his mouth on hers, she'd nearly spilled the bucket of stain all over the lobby floor today because the memory of them on the grass in her front yard from earlier in the week had changed to them lying naked on the floor in the theater. Now here he was planting his mouth on hers. Again! *And, whew!* She fanned her face. *His lips are amazing.*

Her stomach and her emotions were doing constant flip-flops. He could have her go from annoyed to embarrassed to furious to shocked to curiously charmed and happy all in ten seconds flat. And lust simmered underneath her emotions. She looked at the dinner on her lap. Mmm, Katie did make the best pasta salad and fried chicken. And she hadn't eaten much all day. God, she loved food. She needed to be better about eating during the day if the grumpy, embarrassing growl of her stomach was any indication. It was always her intention, to eat better, to pack healthy lunches. She just never seemed to follow through. Too many other things to check off her lists.

I'll just have a bite. The pasta burst with flavor. Lemon, pepper, fresh-from-the-garden sweet tomatoes.

When she looked up, Turner was back, another couple of beers and something else she couldn't see in his hand. He sat back down beside her and smiled. "It's good isn't it?"

"The best," Lily said and devoured another bite.

"Did you just agree with me?" Turner feigned shock and handed her a beer.

A grin snuck across her face before she could stop it. "It's hard to argue about Katie's cooking."

"True," he said. His laser-beam eyes studied her. "I've missed it." He took a piece of chicken from the bowl and settled in next to her. The evening swirled around them. Hot and dry, a nice breeze.

Had he really missed his mother's cooking? Had he missed anything else? *Anyone* else? Her emotional bouncy ball was exhausting. Too many curious questions. Then there was his nearness. His shoulder touching hers, their thighs rubbing up against each other. Every spot on her body screamed with desire for him. Did he feel it too?

"I called Premier today."

"What…I mean why?" She was caught off guard again.

"Because I had a bad feeling too. And Cruz asked me to follow up with it since he's in the middle of wedding madness. It's my responsibility, anyway."

"A feeling, huh? You're not just mocking me?"

He caught her gaze in his. "I don't go around mocking people, especially intelligent, talented, beautiful women I'm sharing a meal with."

And wishing he could get into bed, she thought. Her body was on a high cliff waiting to dive off at the thought of them in bed together, naked, hot, soft and hard, all those muscles of his hers to possess.

Holy hell. She held the beer bottle up to her flaming cheek. And he smiled as though he knew exactly what she was thinking.

"I understand real estate and development possibly better than you, Lily." That shot her lusty thoughts out of her mind. "And we both know it involves more than land and money. Passions often play the major role, motivating people into behaving irrationally."

"My father and I are not acting irrationally," she said, anger in her voice, trying to hide the hurt of his accusation.

"I wasn't talking about you, or your father, Liliana." Turner placed his hand on her knee gently. She called him snobby and grumped about his enormous ego, but he'd shown her tenderness. More than once, now. That was something she'd never imagined in all the years she'd dreamed of him, that he could be tender. Or how much it made her heart feel like it had bird's wings and could take flight. That he would catch her if she fell.

She wanted desperately to believe him.

She took a long sip of her beer. "Sorry, I... My emotions tend to rule my mouth some of the time."

"Some of the time?" His lips twitched, melting her and frustrating her, depending on her mood. "It's refreshing, your bold honesty. Anyway, and, don't bite my head off, but I'd like to help you."

"Why?" Her voice was quieter.

"Legally, if the properties are mine, I need to figure out the mess."

The salty bite of chicken got stuck in her throat. *Right, he owns them now.* Big-time developer Turner Brockman owned half of Graciella. He might own her hardware store, one more piece of her heart. She tried to fight back the panic when he continued.

"And because I also don't like the smell of things. Because no real estate agent in their right mind would be ignoring calls to interested buyers in a hot area like Graciella, unless something was wrong. Because you intrigue me, and because I can't keep my mind off you. Brownie?" He offered with an open, casual smile.

Damn it! He did it again. He lured her in with his voice, calling her intelligent and beautiful. The voice that seduced with its cadence, with his admissions. She didn't know which captivated her more, that he believed her or that he wanted her. Then, when she was melting from the heat, he changed course to...brownies!

Turner teased her, fed her, listened to her, acted like he wanted to know her. But what about the town, would he want to know Graciella too, the way she did, the way the people here did, in a way that said they cherished it? Maybe he was doing her a favor by changing the subject to chocolate.

"Anyone who doesn't appreciate these doesn't rate in my book." She took the biggest one he offered.

"Where do I rate in your book, Lily?" He set his beer down and leaned back on his arm. Settling his gaze on her face, he replaced his casual smile with that open look of hunger. Caught, Lily tried to read what she saw written deep in his eyes. Her heart was doing its own search and she wondered if he could hear it thumping against her chest.

"I don't know what you mean?" She thrust the bowl back into his lap and stood. "I have work to do," she said.

"Does that mean I have a chance?" Turner called.

"A chance at what, Turner?" she started to call back, but he'd jogged to her before she realized that he'd moved at all.

"At rating in your book?" He stood in front of her so she couldn't avoid him. Arms at his sides, body open to her, eyes full of vulnerability. It stopped her heart and without thought, she reached up to put her hand on his chest.

"I…" But before she could finish, he held her hand tight against his body and placed his lips gently to hers. He caressed like the warm breeze, his tongue asking to be let in, and her whole body tuned into his lips. *Why isn't he touching me everywhere?* She melted into him, to the heat that burned between them.

"Lily," he said in that deep voice that tightened the coil of need in her belly.

"Yes." She closed her eyes, lost herself in the scent of him, freshly showered, his hair still damp. Musky roses lining the fences sent their bloom into the evening air.

"I want you." Words and desire hummed against her.

Lily pulled away abruptly, but she made the mistake of looking into his eyes. They burned with desire. *Honest and raw.* Her throat was suddenly dry. Want and fear twisted inside her. Without warning, tears filled her eyes and she knew she had to get away.

"I have to go. I...I need to visit my father."

Chapter Thirteen

She was the most infuriating woman he'd ever met. There were so many facets to her that he wanted to learn, to know. Her passion, her desires, her anger. Why she melted into him with such openness, then so abruptly pulled away and shuttered herself from him.

Each time he kissed her, he could feel her desire in the way her body responded, the shiver that went through her, how she arched toward him. She might think of it as a surrender, as a letting down of the guard she was so determined to keep up, but he knew it for what it was — grabbing the reins and diving in full speed. He wanted her to see that. Instead she scrambled away. Every time.

Oh, hell! He remembered what Adam had mentioned about the Alzheimer's diagnosis. He'd been an ass. Not only had he not asked about her father tonight while they shared chicken and beer, he'd been annoyed that she'd left him standing here so she could go visit the man. And the tears in her eyes when she'd left had sliced him open. Fuck, he was blind sometimes. If he intended to know everything about her, he'd start by asking about her father. In fact, he'd go after her and ask her tonight, check on her. As much as he wanted her body, he wanted her mind, her heart, her trust too. And to care for her. That was another first.

He'd have to be stealth-like. Or who knew what would happen the next time he fed her hungry stomach. If independent, stubborn Liliana caught on to his actions, she might dump the pasta salad on his head.

Warm and lovely to everyone around her, she'd been like a feral cat to him from that first day. Not that he wanted to dampen her spirit, but he was confused by how much she seemed to hate him. *Mmm, she certainly doesn't hate kissing you. At least until she realizes she's enjoying it.*

What underlying current was he missing?

The other day when he'd driven her home and she'd jumped down his throat for being gone twelve years, she hadn't been incorrect in what she'd said. And it had hit him like a punch. But it had felt more like a sucker punch than one deserved. He *had* disappeared for twelve years and he *had* been a miserable son and brother, but the lashing hadn't felt right coming from her. There was something else underneath her ire.

This morning, when he'd asked about the hardware store, she'd immediately assumed he'd been patronizing her. Even tonight when he'd mentioned one of his reasons for wanting to help her and her father was because he'd inherited whatever T.D. owned in Graciella, he'd seen the quick blanch of fear and pain on her face, as though he'd physically hit her.

Approaching her house, Turner found he was no longer smiling. He would never hit her or, for that matter, hurt her unknowingly in any way. The only thing he'd ever hit was his punching bag, even when he'd wanted to take out his frustration on his father.

But he had put fear and hurt in her. How? Why did she hate him? He beat her home, sat in one of her porch chairs and, while he waited, took the time to calm his own emotions. She'd be pissed, *again*, to find him there, but maybe she'd finally give him an explanation.

Sucking back her tears, Lily drove without crying. More than anything, her heart felt heavy. Finally, what she'd secretly longed for in her girlhood dreams, Turner Brockman's desire. One small phrase, '*I want you*,' had shattered her. There would be no such thing as control. Not when he was touching her, kissing her. Whatever had made her think an affair with him would be rational disintegrated in his powerful words. There was no way she could be with Turner Brockman, then *get over him*.

She wasn't willing to risk breaking her heart over again for a night of passion with Turner. He might want her, but that was no longer enough. *He has to want all of this*, she thought, as she curved up the hills and looked over the farmland to the ocean beyond. *He has to want the life here, a slower pace of life in the country.* But this wasn't his dream. Lily didn't even know if the lure of owning property could keep him here. If his past was any indication, he had no interest in the charm of the downtown. Especially a downtown he cared nothing for. Turner Brockman's career history boasted not one ounce of charm or legacy. Nope, he demolished those with each project he acquired. He was the exact opposite of everything she stood for.

Her father was awake and flashed a look her way then went back to his movie. *Not even a glimmer of recognition in his features.* It both saddened her and lifted the feeling of burden, because her mind was a muddled mess anyway. For once she was relieved in a bittersweet way that her papá couldn't see her like this. But tonight was the only time he'd been awake when she'd visited this week. He slept most of the time now. It was normal in this stage of the disease, the nurses had told her. Normal and disease were two words Lily would never put together.

Damn Turner Brockman and his annoying return visit! Damn him! Lily didn't have time for her thoughts to be in a tangled mess, her emotions flittering around inside her like…like before. A girl with hope blooming in her young heart. She had a business to run, work to do and a father to take care of or at least manage to visit during the hour or two he was conscious each day. Although she couldn't blame Turner for her father not recognizing her anymore.

Lily was too busy cursing the demon Alzheimer's as she climbed her porch steps that she didn't see Turner leaning against her porch railing when she pulled up. With her hat pulled low and her concentration shot, she smacked into him.

"Jesus, Turner! You scared the hell out of me!" Lily said, fumbling back. "What are you doing here?" She pulled her hat back down and brushed past him into her house. She could feel his stare on her back. "Well?" she demanded, whirling around. It wasn't a fair fight if she couldn't see him. Or maybe she should run and hide. His eyes beat any weapon she had.

"Solving some puzzles," he finally said.

"Puzzles?" *What in the hell is that supposed to mean?*

"Tell me why you hate me so much, Lily. Let's start there. It should be easy since you're spilling over with animosity aimed specifically at me."

She didn't look away. The man was brave. She'd give him that. Brave or stupid. Hate wasn't the word she would use to describe her feelings, but she honestly didn't know what to tell him, what she felt *comfortable* telling him. She was exposed under his gaze, and for once in her life that feeling made her shaky and uncomfortable because it involved him. Pissed was more like it. She was still pissed off at the way he'd treated her all those years ago like an idiotic female. Like she'd asked to be attacked. Pissed that he'd returned only to eventually leave again. Pissed that no matter how much her mind ordered her body not to want him, her body laughed at her.

Pissed that her heart still longed for him.

"Lily?"

"Hate's a pretty strong word."

"What word would you use to describe why every time I'm around you, you look like you'd love nothing more than to punch me?"

"Because I would," she said then slapped her hand over her mouth. "I can't believe I said that out loud."

"Now we're getting somewhere." Turner's frame relaxed a smidgen. "Why?"

"I don't know." No way in hell was she going to bare her feelings to him.

"Liar," he said. "I see a story raging in those mysterious beautiful eyes of yours. I just don't know the details."

Desire, confusion, sadness, need, loneliness all beat into her. She put her hands over her eyes and tried to rub the ache from them. "I can't do this right now, Turner. I'm exhausted and dirty and my emotions are…" She moved her hands from her eyes. He was there rubbing her arms. Instead of desire, his face was full of concern.

"How's your father? I meant to ask you earlier, but I got distracted by your eyes." His voice was gentle, like his touch on her arms, soothing, warming. It undid her. Giving in, she faceplanted into his chest and luxuriated in the feel of his confident arms holding her, the caress of his fingers on her back. She let her tears fall then. Tears she'd been holding back for a year now at her father's deterioration, at his inability to recognize her anymore, at the knowledge that he could live for years sinking farther away from her. She'd barely cried since his diagnosis, because she'd spent the last year being angry and shocked by this disease that had ravaged him. She'd kept her shit together in order to get things done. She hadn't made time for tears. At this strange moment in these warm arms, her emotions on edge, she let go and let him comfort her.

She turned her head to the side to hear Turner's heartbeat. "He doesn't know me anymore," she whispered. "And I don't know him. We're strangers, the two of us. He's all I have left, but his light is gone, his humor, his passion for life, all gone."

Turner tightened his hold and listened. She appreciated his silence because she didn't think she could bear any words of sympathy. When the tears finally stopped, she lifted her head. "I got your shirt all wet."

"I think I'll live." There wasn't any pity in his eyes, and she was grateful for that too.

She reached up on her tiptoes and kissed his cheek. "Thank you. I'm sure that's not what you expected when you came over here."

"I never know what to expect with you, Lily." He held her head in his hands and wiped tears off her cheeks with his thumbs. "I came over here to talk to you. To care for you. I came over here to find out why you can't stand me. I came over here to convince you to let me make love to you."

He wants to care for me? "You did?" she said on a sigh.

"Mmm hmm."

He kissed her breathless. She opened, wanting to be wrapped in his heat. Truly, one kiss from this man and she was a puddle of lust. He trailed his lips down the column of her neck, whispering secrets to her, so softly. "But now's not the right time." He placed one featherlight caress over her heart, pulled his mouth away and all she felt was loss.

"It's not?" *It is. It's the exact right time. My defenses are shot. Have your way with me. I need you.*

"You know I want you. I know you want me. But your heart is hurting and I would be taking advantage of you."

"You would?" *Take advantage. Please.* Did she have to beg? What had happened to her? Weak from his light touch on her cheeks, the soft skin of her neck. He'd kissed her *heart*. She'd lost all sense of thought, or reason. She wanted him to keep kissing her everywhere.

He walked toward the door. He was going to leave her here like this, all flustered and hot and wanting? *No, no, no!* She didn't know whether to admire his honorable character or throw things at him for leaving. Extremely heavy breakable things.

"Goodnight, Liliana."

"Turner." All the fury was back in her voice. How dare he *'Liliana'* her when he was leaving her panting?

"Yes."

"Don't think this means my desire to punch you has disappeared."

He flashed his magnificent predatory grin at her. "Don't think this means I'll stop trying to figure out why you want to. Sleep tight."

Chapter Fourteen

Maybe Turner should have been more directly involved with the construction at Brockman House, but as much as he liked riling Lily up, he did not intend to step on her pretty toes. Besides, he grinned, he intended to save all his micromanaging for when he got her naked.

Plus her crew did phenomenal work. All that didn't mean he couldn't check things out daily. He was extremely interested in the build. And it was an excellent excuse to check out his woman too. She might not know she was his yet, but he had every intention of heading them both in that direction. Because he didn't just want her, he wanted to belong to her too. Together, connected, bound to each other. *Love.* He sought all of that now, with Lily.

And damn, but he did not expect to see her on the three-story roof of the north wing one Thursday morning. He had to bite back the cursing he wanted to hurl at her. He'd been giving her a bit of space since she'd opened up about her father, but keeping his eye on her. That did not mean he wanted to keep his eye on her while she strolled across the peak, and possibly fell and broke that gorgeous neck of hers. Jesus, his heart stopped.

The sun was hardly up, but his goddess was. High above everyone, standing tall, giving orders, or more like perfect suggestions that her mostly male crew listened to and followed without question. He found his breath that had lodged in his throat, stopped himself from demanding she get the hell down and instead watched her in action. She could have been safe, on the ground, rolling out the sheets of painted steel for the metal roof. Not Liliana. She was right there in the mess of work as they caught each piece and screwed them into place. Directing, working, laughing.

A metal roof was smart. Expensive, but efficient and long-lasting. It would add a nice look to the place too, during sunset as the sun's fading rays bounced off the deep red color, shooting streaks of fire across the land, exactly like she did. *Streaks of fire.*

He waited till she was finally back on solid ground before he spoke to her. No sense sending her temper spinning while she balanced thirty feet in the air. He wasn't certain he could keep his own in check at knowing she was up there. If he opened his mouth, he might curse up a storm.

"Metal roof, huh?"

Her spine stiffened before she turned in his direction. She stood under one of the tents, marking things on her clipboard with one hand and shoving a donut into her mouth with the other. Without giving her a chance to answer, he gave her sugary lips a gentle kiss and set a warm mug of coffee in her hand.

"Good choice," he said, taking advantage while her mouth was full of food and her eyes discombobulated. "Most people would take the cheap way out. End up having to re-roof in less than a decade. I approve." And before she could say anything, which was indeed rare for her, he left her to work out his restlessness on the new barn his brothers were building. Far away from her sexy, sweet lips and sharp tongue that were sure to get him trouble.

* * * *

Turner and his brothers sat on the fence to watch the horses in the late afternoon. Since Turner had been back, the three had met often at the horse pasture after a day's work to catch up. Turner had just showered, after looking and feeling like he'd wrestled a pig in the mud.

"Feels good, doesn't it?" Adam said. "A hard day's work."

"Speak for yourself." Turner practically groaned at the ache in his shoulders from carrying and lifting beams

"That outta shape, huh?" Adam teased.

"Shut up. No one's ever in shape to build half a barn in a day."

"Admit it," Cruz said, opening a beer for each of them. "You loved it."

"Nope. Not using the word love for that." But Turner smiled. He didn't know how to say the words yet, but it felt great to be here with his brothers. He'd had no idea how much he missed them.

"So, are you going to make a move or not?" Cruz asked.

"Make a move?" Turner asked.

"He's talking about Lily, you idiot," Adam said.

Turner choked on his beer. "Excuse me?" He jumped down from the fence.

"Can't play stupid with us." Cruz laughed. "We all noticed your tongue hanging out of your mouth the night Lily showed up for dinner. Plus, Miranda saw you giving her a ride into town the other day. And none of us miss how you seek her out on the north wing."

"You can't tell us you don't think she's gorgeous. Then we'd have to have your head examined," Adam said.

"Why haven't you made a move then, little brother?" *Shit!* His stomach dropped. Maybe Lily and Adam already had something going.

Adam laughed. "You should see your face, Turner. That look says it all. Lily and I are friends. She's always been an annoying big sister to me, nothing more."

"So," Cruz prodded.

Relieved and happy, Turner grinned at his brothers, completely at ease and enjoying himself. "For some reason, she absolutely hates my guts."

Cruz barked out a laugh. "You're not going to let that get in your way, are you?"

"Nope." Turner finished his beer. "She's even more beautiful when she's pissed off at me."

"Should I ask you what your intentions are?" Adam said. "She's special, Turner. She's a complete romantic, a dreamer. She wants it all."

Adam's words were heavy, but surprisingly they didn't scare the crap out of Turner. He looked at his brothers. Good men, both of them. And he was proud to be related to them instead of full of shame for his connection to T.D. So many weights had felt lifted from his chest since he'd been back, since they'd welcomed him back. He hadn't expected to stay very long, hadn't expected to *want* to stay. Every day he felt better, more settled. He slept dreamless, deep sleeps. And Lily? She'd affected him more than any woman, any experience in his life. "Let's just say I'm very interested and I plan to find out if she feels the same."

"Speak of the devil." Adam nodded at the pasture leading to one of the workers' cottages. Lily was dragging the shop vac from her truck into the cottage.

Turner hesitated a moment, watching her. "I should see if she needs help," he said. He handed his beer to Cruz and headed in Lily's direction. He turned once and said, "Feels good to be back." And it did, he thought, following the path that led straight to the bonfire, his bonfire.

The cottage was empty of furniture. Hardwood floors, newly restored and shining, stretched out to the kitchen and back deck overlooking the cliff to the ocean. Afternoon sun warmed the main room. Rays streaked through the windowpanes and shimmered over Lily. Damn, she even made vacuuming look good. And he loved watching her when she was lost in her thoughts, completely caught off guard.

"Hey," he said. "Want some help?" Surprise rolled through her features. She quickly shot her guards back up, those walls that should scare him the hell away but that he couldn't seem to get enough of. Maybe because he could feel the passion simmering behind them. And Turner wanted nothing more than to find a way to the heart of the woman.

What in the hell is he thinking, turning up everywhere I am? And oh, she'd been *thinking* of him, thinking of that kiss in her living room. How he'd told her he wanted to make love to her, then left her wanting. Her entire body had been restless and edgy since that evening, and her mind had been all shredded paper. Sleep was nonexistent. She hadn't had time to work on the theater all week and she didn't dare work on the north wing surrounded by people who might be able to see her in complete turmoil after yesterday morning. How dare he kiss her in front of her crew? Bring her *coffee*? She might have jumped his bones if he hadn't offered his *approval* of the roof. Approval her ass. Was he going to start dictating how they built the new wing now that he was home and *interested*? Would he take over? He hadn't shown any sign of that, yet. More like riling her up on purpose. *The nerve.* After racing around like a crazy person, she'd picked one of the cottages to work on by herself this evening, hidden. And here he was again.

He took the shop vac out of her hands and continued the slow path across the floor. "How are you feeling today?"

"Fine?"

Turner laughed. "Are you sure about that?"

Absolutely not. "Yes. I'm fine, why?" She couldn't help snapping at him.

"Because I care about you."

Dammit, he was being considerate and caring again. Chipping away at her defenses little by little. It all had her on edge, his kindness, his desire, her pent-up feelings toward him.

She gulped cold water from her bottle, trying to concentrate on anything besides Turner. Trying to control how she ached when he was near. The man was infinitely more dangerous to her system than the broody teenager had ever been.

"Want to finish our conversation from the other night, Liliana?" He switched off the vacuum.

"What conversation?"

"Playing stupid doesn't suit you. It contradicts the fire in those gorgeous eyes of yours."

She snapped her head around. "Did you learn how to compliment a girl in the corporate world, or does that grace come naturally to you?"

Turner walked toward her slowly. Too slowly. Backed her against the island and pulled her cap off. "Sarcasm doesn't suit you either."

"How do you know what the hell suits me?" Lily fired back, her temper exploding. "You…"

Turner put his fingers on her lips, but that was all it took to silence her. Hell, she practically melted at his touch. Such a wonderful touch. She wanted to reach her tongue out and taste his fingers. Maybe bite him too. Just a little.

"Let's start over. First, I kissed you like this." Turner captured her mouth with his, caressed her shoulders and urged the kiss deeper. His clean soapy scent invaded her body, she wanted to climb onto him and never let go.

"I've told you I wanted you. Now you say what's written all over your face, 'I want you too, Turner.'"

Lily ignored his words and pulled his head back down to meet hers, lighting them both on fire.

"Say it, Lily." Turner whispered his seduction in her ear. "I need to hear you say it." His fingers trailed across her neck and her collarbone. His lips hovered right underneath her ear.

And she was lost in a way that had never felt so glorious. "I want you too, Turner." *I've wanted you forever.*

Turner kissed the soft skin under her ear, then traded kisses for sweet words. "What you do to me." He dragged his mouth down her neck, making her moan. "The way your body reaches for mine. Those sounds you make, God, Lily." He took control of her mouth in a way she didn't understand. Where was the speed, the frenzy from before? This time he played her body like she was the stone and he the sculptor, gracefully giving each facet attention. He kissed her with reverence, melting his lips to hers. She fluttered closer. His hands cradled her head, molding her to his specific desire. Slowly he dipped his tongue inside, darting in and out. Each new way he tasted her quickened her breath and the tingles shooting all over her skin. She wanted to do the same to him, cherish his lips, but she could barely hold herself up, let alone make intelligent sensual decisions. So she allowed herself to be ravaged.

With his lips still devouring hers, he danced his fingers down her neck and back to her shoulders. Undoing the buttons on her shirt, he slid it off. It might have taken him a year for the time he took in doing so. The touch of his bare fingers on her arms as he moved the material down, down, until it disappeared altogether. *Shirt? Who needs a shirt? Why shirts?* She wanted to arch out of the rest of her clothes and rub her body against his. She was dizzy, languid and needy.

Desire raced through her and she couldn't get enough of his hot skin, his hungry mouth. His body behaved the same. She could feel the ripples coming off him, even while he tried to hold them at bay. He lifted her to the island and finally left her lips to anoint more of her body with his hungry kisses. First her neck. *Yes, please kiss my neck!* It was as though her neck was made for him. So many spots to arouse her. Then down to her breasts. He trailed his fingers gently over the line of her bra, his gaze lost in some dream of his own.

Finally he cut the leash on his desires, ripped her bra down and sucked her sensitive flesh into his mouth. Oh, God, his mouth. She arched her body to him and held on to his head. He made quick work of the rest of her clothes. Her fingers shook, undoing Turner's buttons. Faster, why couldn't she go faster? She wanted to touch every inch of his skin. *So much for reverence. So much for control.*

Starving, empty, with a need to be filled, they devoured each other.

He drank her body in, sampling everywhere. He possessed her with his hands. She soared. She could barely function in this glorious high long enough to concentrate on him, but she did. It was imperative that she touch him, that she *feel* him. This one time she allowed her hands to dream. With her eyes closed, she sketched his body in her mind, his wide strong shoulders pulsing with a rhythm she allowed herself to believe he drew from her body, down his narrow torso. She pushed at his jeans with her bare feet. Lily loved the feel of his skin, hot and comforting at the same time. His abdomen full of muscles, strong legs, long-fingered hands that climbed around her, hungering for more of her to caress, to knead, to discover.

Aroused, wanting, tingling, she moaned when he parted her thighs with his hand and touched her where she ached to be connected to him.

"Turner." Glorious shocks raced through her body.

"There are so many things I want to do to you." Turner's voice had lost the soft, seductive caress. Sharp gravel laced his words. "Tried to take my time. I don't think I can wait, Lily. What you do to me. What we do to each other." Turner dragged her body to the edge, as if they could become one.

Well, they could and, oh, she wanted to.

"Yes," she breathed back. "I need you, Turner."

With her words spoken, they fumbled their way to the floor. While he grabbed a condom out of his jeans, she kissed his chest and grazed her fingers over him, feeling each plane, each dip, each hard muscle. When he arranged her on his lap and plunged up into her body in one strong thrust, she came apart instantly. Oh, yes, this was what she wanted. She felt him coming undone inside her in waves. Wrapped around each other, they held tight. Turner whispered her name again and again as they rose and gentled together.

"Wow," she said, the sound raspy. Apparently, fabulous sex took her voice away.

His laughter shook both their bodies and she loved that rumble against her lightning-struck skin. He hadn't let her go. And her heart beat like crazy everywhere, in her belly, in the tips of her fingers, in her eyes. Eyes that wanted to drift off into sleep and dream of Turner, his heart galloping next to hers. He'd been as affected, as shattered as she had.

"I expected nothing less," he said with his cocky attitude. He tumbled them gently to the side, still connected physically. And though she should have laughed with him, agreed with him, for some unknown reason, his words sliced her raw. He was so certain of everything and she was a mess.

"Mmm," she said, choking back her fear. He took her hand with one of his warm ones and used the other to reach for her clothes. Lazy, beyond the horizon, the sun took with it the heat of the day. He surprised her again by fastening her bra around her, then buttoning her shirt and kissing her skin right above the top button. "So beautiful," he said, that reverence back in his voice.

No. Stop. She didn't want to hear him say nice things. She didn't want to hear anything he might regret or worse, that might linger inside her long after he'd left town. It felt like digging through boulders to pretend confidence enough to get out of there, to get away from him.

"It's a good thing there's no bed in here. I might never let you leave." His fingers sent sparks through her as he pulled her pants slowly up her body. The look in his eyes was one of awe. His smile, so happy.

Her heart fell for him all over again and she was going to start crying. *Again* with the tears in front of him. *No.* She'd already cried as a girl for him. She'd cried alone when thinking of him. She'd even cried on him over her father. But this was different. This would be a complete coming apart, because this time the tears would be over the fact that he would never be hers.

"Lily," he said with concern. "What's wrong? You went from shimmering to ghost pale in a matter of seconds." He rubbed her hands in his. "You're afraid, aren't you?" There was no smug accusation in his tone. Only confusion and care, which somehow made it worse. With each rock she built up against him, he smashed it down with everything she could ever want, and everything she could never have, not from him.

She shook her head and struggled to breathe. "No, I can't...I have to go, Turner." She grabbed her hat and her keys and ran, leaving him standing there naked, calling her name.

Chapter Fifteen

Stunned and confused as hell, Turner watched her fly away. Such an ordinary word, away, and yet there was nothing easy about the way he was feeling right now at once more watching her go *away* from him. A flat-out panic run. He might have been annoyed, but the vulnerable look on her face had shaken him. Shit, he was annoyed too. Was it what had just happened that had made her freak out? Or that he'd called her out on her emotions, her fear? He hadn't mean to be an ass.

He wanted to pull her back, to hold her tightly, to lift her up and carry her with him somewhere private and safe where he could convince her they should be together. Where they could convince each other. Turner's desire had a mind all of its own. Or perhaps he had no mind left whatsoever. Every time he kissed her, tasted her scent, drowned in her vibrancy, marveled at her intelligence, reveled in her temper, he wanted all of her. There was a stirring inside him, something growing. He wanted more than her body — he wanted to know her soul.

He took a walk down the rocky path to the beach. He'd thought to walk alone, shake off this edgy feeling he was left with every time she gave him that terrified look and escaped. But Javier was on the beach with one of the horses, letting it play and gallop, tease the water with its nose. Always, the horse returned to Javier. For approval? For love? Turner didn't know. It was a beautiful sight to witness, either way. The man had a way with horses.

When Turner got closer, the horse noticed him and whinnied her massive head in greeting. Javier waved him over. "Turner, perfect. I needed help and you arrived. Here." He handed the reins to him. "Buttermilk has something in her shoe. Hold her for me while I take a look."

"She likes the water?" Turner asked Javier while holding the large mare steady.

"Indeed. I've never seen a horse so taken with the waves. I thought I'd trick her into playing while I looked at her hoof. Turns out I'm not as savvy as that."

"She's a beauty." Her light flaxen mane — in contrast to her deep chestnut body — teased around her eyes.

"Yes, but skittish with her heart. She likes *you*. I see."

"Are we still talking about Buttermilk?" Turner asked.

"Depends on if you need someone to talk to."

The water was choppy in the breeze, but brilliant with the sun's rays stretching low over its surface. Slowly, like a salve, all these kind people and happy feelings had taken over his gut-wrenching memories of this place. In his personal battle between the good and bad, the good was acing it. Ah, hell, he wanted to grab hold and never let go. "Skittish isn't the word I'd used for Lily's heart, more like hidden deep underground in the catacombs." *Kind of like my own heart when I first left Graciella.*

"If you're paying attention, which I think you are, you'll see she's only worried about her heart when it comes to you and your intentions. To the rest of us, her heart's an open book, full of love and kindness."

"She trusts you," Turner said.

Javier nodded and gently set the horse's leg down. "A small flare," Javier cooed to Buttermilk and took the reins from Turner.

"Can you fix it?"

"Sure we can, with time, patience and a combination of techniques."

Sounds exactly like what I need when it comes to Lily.

"I guess you need to figure out what your intentions are, son."

Lily. She'd seared into his being and he couldn't get her out, and he found, along the wide flat coast, with the meditation of the waves, that he didn't want to. Was this what it felt like to let someone into his heart? Hell, he'd buried his heart so long ago, he didn't recognize the feeling. *Isn't that embarrassing?*

"I want to make a home in Graciella with my family and with Lily."

"Perhaps that's what she wants too." Javier winked at him and headed up the path to the barns.

I wish, Turner thought. But damn if she wasn't intent on shoving him away. He was determined to get through Lily's angry exterior, to fully know her. To make her believe that he wanted not just her gorgeous body, but to possess all of her. The way she already possessed him. It came down to trust. And he needed to gain hers, to build a strong enough foundation for her to feel secure.

He would solve the real estate issue and hopefully, in doing so, give Lily back her birthright. He felt both clueless and lightheaded at the thrill of piecing everything together. Somehow, he had to show her he wanted to cherish her, that what was important to her, mattered to him. Would she trust him then?

As the sun's last rays set the sky to pink fire, he thought of the flames in Lily's eyes, how sometimes they were simmering coals, and other times sparklers on the Fourth of July, to the full inferno in them when he kissed her. It was her eyes. They'd cast a spell on him. Logic told him there was no such thing, but staring into them, a man could find himself lost forever. They spoke of boldness, and power, beauty and mesmerizing things, like the waves before him. There it was in his chest and his gut, the deep rumble he felt. It was for her, and it was unbelievable.

Maybe Liliana Moreno, strong, independent goddess and romantic, needed to be courted. *'Time, patience and a combination of techniques.'* And he laughed thinking of ways he could surprise her with his courting. He knew she wouldn't expect it. And, boy, how much fun it was going to be to see her reactions.

Chapter Sixteen

It wasn't that she was trying to avoid Turner over the next few days. She needed to think, which was impossible around his lips. Already she was in rough seas where her heart was concerned. She wanted to stay pissed at him, but he kept surprising her with his gentle kindness when she needed it, his insistence on helping her, his dreamy caresses. Flat out telling her he wanted her. Appearing out of nowhere and taking her with a hunger she'd never felt from a man before. No, not just hunger, intense concentration on her.

She wanted to fly with the euphoria he lit inside her. Instead she felt like weeping for how confused she was. How could she fall in love with him all over again when he'd never planned to stay? And yet it felt out of her hands, her path set out in front of her, leading her to him. Lily more than directed her own way — she carved it out in front of her. Giving even one ounce over to another felt like giving up a part of herself, like defeat.

But in Turner's arms, defeat was the last thing she thought of.

Luckily, with all the construction work, repairs at the barns, stupid real estate fiascos and a wedding in the works this summer, she and Turner both had plenty to keep them busy. Even though he hadn't shown up to surprise her anywhere in eight days—because of course she was counting, dammit—he still seemed to be everywhere.

He was helping Cruz and Adam work on the new milking machine when she went to find Javier Monday evening. And watching the three handsome brothers with toolbelts assemble heavy equipment, she'd forgotten why the heck she was there in the first place.

She'd caught sight of his backside repairing one of the fences that butted up against the horse paddocks yesterday and tripped at that sight. From the ladder where she stood painting shutters on the cottages, his and Adam's laughter pulled her gaze. And there he was in the fading sunlight, shirtless, sweat covering the muscles on his back, the sky a dusky blue behind him.. He and Adam laughed and teased each other, but his back was all she could think about. How this was the first time she'd seen his back from this perfect view, uncovered. Strong corded muscles lifting heavy pieces of wood. The glorious way his skin would feel under her touch. How she wanted to sketch that back, preferably while he slept, naked, in her bed.

Then there were the times she hadn't seen him, but felt his…warmth, comfort, seduction? She didn't know what the heck to label it. Every night since he'd ravished her body in the cottage, he'd left flowers on her doorstep. A small bouquet of barely pink old-fashioned roses one night. Brilliant fiery-orange dahlias another. And last night, one single blood-red lily. There'd been no notes, but she'd known. Lily surrounded herself with flowers, could pick a bouquet whenever she wanted, but to have Turner go out of his way to intentionally bring her beauty made her blush with feeling cherished, seen. Silly, she'd started looking forward to them.

Then there were the pastries. Every morning when she got to her truck, there was a pastry waiting for her in a pretty pink bakery box. He'd caught on to her sweet tooth. And not only had he noticed, he didn't criticize or lecture, but fed her. And he must have risen early to sneak to her house before she woke.

Three times she'd caught him studying the architectural plans for Brockman House with Miranda and smiling at what he saw, as though he actually did approve. That word, he'd used it to annoy her in regard to the metal roof, before he handed her the best cup of coffee she'd ever tasted. But secretly, as with her house, she wanted his approval, wanted him to love her work. And there was no way in hell she'd ask his opinion. So instead of approaching him, she'd dug in deep with the labor, wiring, staining the new front steps, or her safest place far from Turner, working on the skylights high on the roof.

The man was seducing her, and hell, he was doing it without words or the use of his body, without that killer grin or his amazing lips. Sneaky bastard.

Was she surprised when she arrived at the north wing Friday afternoon to find him wielding a nail gun and installing baseboards and trim with her crew? Well, surprise wasn't exactly what she'd call it. More like being electrocuted with a jolt of lust. The man was so insanely gorgeous in jeans and a T-shirt with his dark hair barely curling near the ends. The serious look on his face as he measured and aligned. *Mmm, he can measure and align me.* She watched him nail a piece in place, then run his fingers smoothly over the wood, almost reverently. The way she wanted him to run his hands over her body. She ached.

"Hey!"

Lily yelled at the elbow jab to her side. "What was that for?"

"Making sure you're alive," Miranda said.

"What?" Lily looked at her, absolutely confused.

"Afternoon, Lily." Turner's voice carried over the noise of the construction. Warm and deep, it zapped through her. "Miranda," he said.

Lily snapped her gaze back in his direction. His grin spread out over his face, then he turned and ignored her.

"I was talking to you, asking you questions, and you were silent, which is a first, I think. Lost in some other world far away from here." Miranda glanced in Turner's direction, then found Lily's eyes again. "Tell me, was it a delicious thought you were lost in?" she whispered and nudged Lily again, gently this time.

"You have bony elbows." Lily frowned.

At that Miranda laughed. "I've also never known *you* to change the subject."

"I'm not changing the subject. What subject? We weren't even *on* a subject."

"Mmm hmm." Miranda smiled and leaned against the doorway.

"Why is everyone so smug lately?" For an instant she snuck one more quick look at Turner. *Is he sexier in jeans or in his fancy suits? Hmm, neither. Naked like Michelangelo's David.*

"Lily? Hello."

She blinked and hoped there wasn't any drool on her. "Don't you have things to do?" she asked Miranda. "Wedding things or menu planning things or mooning over Cruz things?" Lily waved her hands around Miranda. "Oh, shit!" she said suddenly and took off down the steps. "I forgot about something. I have to go. I'll talk to you later."

Holy crap! She'd been so lost in fantasies about Turner this week she'd nearly forgotten the day and time. She was hosting a surprise shower tonight for Miranda and it was already after three. She had to get her house cleaned and decorated, get herself sparkled up and set the food out. Good thing the girls were coming early to help her. Oh, she was so excited. Miranda had no idea. She'd probably cry her Miranda happy tears. Her friend deserved all the happy tears in the world. She was marrying Cruz and she walked around with a permanent glow from being in love with a wonderful man.

Lily had loved Cruz like a brother her whole life and when Miranda had come to town, Lily had gained a good friend. Now they were going to shower her with a ladies' night of love, delicious food, fun cocktails and sexy gifts. Lily loved surprises almost more than she loved her girlfriends. Tonight would include both.

It was just what she needed. A night without a thought to Turner.

* * * *

Turner nearly ruined the surprise when he walked by the kitchen later and saw Miranda scratching out notes and running her fingers through piles of paperwork.

"Shouldn't you be getting ready for...dinner tonight?" He recovered quickly. Cruz had told Turner about the shower earlier. Said Miranda thought they were going to Lily's for dinner to talk about the wedding. He needed to get her out of the Brockman House kitchen so he could make the pâté he was bringing to her shower.

"Ugh," she sighed. "I keep having ideas for the café menu, then I hate them and start all over. And what I should be doing is checking off wedding lists."

"For someone so frustrated, you sure look happy," he said.

"I am. I can't believe how lucky I am, how much my life has changed in the last few months." She shuffled her notes together. "You're right. I need to get home and get ready. Hey." She smiled. "You should come with us tonight. I don't know why I didn't think of it earlier. We've all been so busy around here we've been neglecting you. It's just me, Cruz and Lily," she said.

He could hear the hint in her voice. The gleam in her eyes were wheels turning, while she subtly tried to matchmake. Turner didn't mind because he had his own plans that included Lily.

"I'd like that," he said and watched the satisfied look in her eyes. Miranda's meddling was going to turn out differently from how she'd intended tonight. And from what everyone said, she was going to absolutely love her evening. "I'll meet you there?" Turner played along with the charade.

As he took the stairs up to his room two at a time, he smiled. Miranda wasn't the only one who was going to be surprised. He couldn't wait to see the look on Lily's face when he arrived at her door.

She might have acted like she'd been avoiding him, but she was a horrible actress. He'd seen her trying *not* to notice him all week. Ever since that evening when she'd opened her body to him, burst his heart into a million amazing pieces, then fled, a skittish new foal. A scowl had animated her face and what a face it was, he thought. Shining, brilliant, fiery, confused. It was like she was writing a novel in her head every time she watched him, trying to figure out the ending. But today when she'd come upon him working on Brockman House, he'd caught a different look on her, a dreamy lost one. Until she realized both he and Miranda had seen her. Then her signature pissed-off attitude had returned. He'd nearly laughed out loud. God, she was fun to watch all flustered and out of sorts. Tonight he planned to *unconfuse* her.

They'd devoured each other, only he wasn't full. More like parched all over again and oddly secure in his desire to spend his life with her. So, while she'd been pretending he was invisible, he'd studied her. He'd taken little steps to pamper her, woo her. He'd done more digging on Premier and all the recent real estate transactions that had taken place in Graciella over the last two years. He'd even worked under her crew on the new wing. And he'd enjoyed all of it. Only he wanted her again with a force he couldn't define.

Turner had never been the bastard his father had been when it came to women, but he hadn't ever been emotionally involved before either. He'd been with women he respected, women he was attracted to, women who wanted absolutely no commitment. Here he was back in Graciella for a few weeks and already

Lily had had his emotions boiling from the minute she'd yelled at him in the street the day he returned. He found he welcomed the upheaval of feelings. He welcomed the challenge of understanding her and, he chuckled, why exactly she wanted to punch him in the face.

* * * *

Turner parked his car in front of Lily's house, knowing it wouldn't ruin Miranda's surprise. Lily's home stood even more beautiful in the evening. Lanterns leading up the path and around her front door were lit. All her windows were covered in curtains, but he could see lights inside. Music and laughter streamed through the front door. He was early, but when he knocked, everything went silent and it took a moment for Lily to come to the door. He was prepared for her fire, his smug smile waiting for her.

And when she opened, he realized there was no such thing as prepared. He wasn't sure who was more surprised. He'd had the breath knocked from him playing sports many times, but he'd never experienced it with such brilliant, instantaneous force. *So much for feeling smug.*

A shimmery wave stood before him. On a hanger, the dress might have looked like a simple sundress. It draped over Lily's lush body and lured like a mesmerizing Caribbean Sea. Fabrics of blues and greens ran together with tiny thin threads of silver sparkling throughout like sunlight sparkling across the water. Fitted on top with two extremely thin straps — straps he wanted to pay very close attention to — straps that snaked over her smooth shoulders. It accentuated all her curves, draped over her hips and flitted below her knees. In strappy silver sandals, she was nearly his height. He dragged his face slowly back up her body. Her curls shimmered too and teased untamed over her ears and strong cheekbones. She'd darkened her eyes and sprinkled some subtle silver shimmery powder around her cheeks, her collarbone, her chest — everywhere. And her mouth opened in such a gorgeous look of shock. It made him feel marginally better about the pounding in his chest.

"Evening," he said.

"What." She pulled him in before slamming the door. "Are. You. Doing. Here?" She simmered with that passion of hers she infused into everything, even dragging him into her house and hissing at him.

"Cruz invited me. I'm going to Miguel's with the guys after Cruz drops Miranda. I made pâté for you ladies and I picked these for you." She took the jar and the bouquet of wildflowers. Before she could pull away, he leaned in, kissed her just below her ear and whispered, "I missed you. You look gorgeous and sinful. I bet you taste even better." He caught the sigh she huffed out at his touch. *Yep, she feels it too.*

He stood back and watched the fire grow molten in her eyes. Desire and annoyance mixing together. Maybe he didn't need to find out why she hated him — this combination of hers was a heady mix.

"Get to the back deck," she ordered. "They should be here any minute." She gave him back the pâté and flowers and hustled him. "Put these on the counter and go outside."

He watched her walk to the front door. The way the fabric swayed and swirled, caressing the backs of her knees with each step of her gorgeous legs in those high,

high heels. God how he wished the shower was over and nothing stood between them. He put his hand to his heart for a minute and welcomed the ache he felt there. Two firsts for him, the ache and the acceptance of it. Would he ever get used to the feeling? Did he want to?

She glanced over her shoulder with one glimpse of that wide-eyed surprised look before she disguised it and waved him back. He let himself out to the deck where several ladies stood beside the pool. An extremely well-designed, seductive, curvy pool surrounded by a cement deck and lush landscape. Pure Lily. Of course, she would have a pool. It was indulgent, luxurious, inviting. *Does she swim naked?* He grew hard at the thought. *Will she invite me to swim with her?*

"Turner," Katie whispered. "What are you doing here?"

"I'm going to Miguel's with the guys," he said. "Roxanna, you look beautiful." She held her sound-asleep baby and swayed from side to side. He introduced himself to the others when Ana grabbed his hand and pulled, so he could crouch down next to her.

"Shh," Ana said. "I hear Uncle Cruz's truck."

He tapped her nose gently with his finger. "I think you're right." He relaxed in the quiet, perfect night. The clear sky overhead held the promise of a party of stars, and he smiled with the other promises it held.

"Surprise!" they yelled when Miranda stepped outside with Cruz and Lily by her side. Miranda's eyes widened, then she laughed and shook her head, as if she couldn't believe what was happening. Turner found Lily watching Miranda, love on her face, a glimmer of tears in her eyes. Some instinct pulled her gaze to him, her face full of emotion. All he could think was that he'd never wanted anything with such force, such commitment. And what Turner Brockman wanted, he got. He hoped that knack didn't fail him now.

"It was Lily's idea," Cruz said and kissed Miranda before the ladies surrounded her.

"You did all this for me?"

"Of course, lady. It was partly selfish. You know how much I love to get dressed up and have a party."

No, she was wrong. He didn't see selfishness in Lily. What he saw was friendship and love. They'd all fallen in love with Miranda, and Turner could see why. Beautiful and full of life, she pulled everyone in with her warmth. She was the kind of person people wanted to give to, to do wonderful things for. There was nothing selfish about this party Lily had planned for Miranda.

A gem, that was what Lily looked like glittering under the lights. Each new angle held something precious. He wanted her in his hands again, uncovering all her angles, exploring every inch of her inside and out.

"You all knew?" Miranda turned to them wiping a tear from her smiling face. "You knew too?" she accused Turner.

"Guilty," he said and gave her a hug.

"Okay, it's time for the men to leave." *Even beautiful when she's bossy. When isn't she beautiful?*

She pushed them out of the front door and leaned up to give Cruz a kiss on the cheek. "Thank you for bringing her."

"We'll see you later," Cruz said.

"Don't I get a kiss and a thank you?" Turner asked. He heard Cruz's hoot of laughter. Turner took her hand, rubbed her fingers gently and loved the way her breath caught. For a moment, she was silent. Then those fire-bright eyes of hers blinked and she pulled back.

"Go," she said and turned back into the house.

"See you later, gorgeous," he whispered after she shut the door in his face.

Chapter Seventeen

Lily leaned back against the door with her eyes closed and tried to steady her breath before joining the girls. She managed to make her breathing feel normal, but her pulse, the way her insides hummed, was a different matter entirely. This was no flutter wings. It was a frenzy beating against a cage, begging to be set free. *My heart.*

She hadn't expected him tonight. Finding him on her doorstep, and the look in his eyes that razed over her body. Eyes starving for her. The smallest, barely-there kiss below her ear. The way his whispered words shivered across her neck, sang all the way inside and made her whole body tingle. How amazing he looked all cleaned up in nice jeans and a black dress shirt with the sleeves rolled to his elbows, the first few buttons undone at the top. How she'd wanted to put her hand right there and touch that dark triangle of skin, drawn by the heat. How easy it would be to forget everyone around them and get lost touching again.

How silly and cute he looked crouched down holding Ana's hand. The soft, delicious burn when he'd held *her* hand. And the feeling of loss inside when she'd separated them. She hadn't expected any of that. For someone who normally loved surprises and excitement and the unknown, Lily was completely out of her element. She forced herself to walk into the kitchen. The flowers he'd brought sat on the counter, a mass of white dahlias, blue phlox, orange and red lilies. They made her smile. *He* made her smile and he confused the hell out of her. She arranged the flowers in a vase, tucked her confusion away and carried a pitcher of daquiris to the warmth of the party.

"Drinks, ladies?" she asked. "Ana, you did a beautiful job setting the table with the candles and flowers. Want to put a little flamingo cocktail straw in each glass after I pour?"

Ana nodded. "I'm so excited you invited me, Lily. I thought Mama would say I was too young."

"You're one of the ladies, honey. And you were one of Miranda's first friends when she came here. Of course you'd be invited. I made you a special smoothie so you can have your own flamingo straw."

"Can I swim? Mama said I could bring my suit. I love swimming in your pool when it's nighttime and the lights are on underwater."

"Absolutely. I'll put the underwater music on too if you want."

"This is so wonderful," Miranda said, taking a cocktail from Lily.

"Let's get this shower started," Roxanna's cousin Gabby said. She and her mother, Mary, uncovered the platters of food. "Lily, it's a sparkly paradise out here with all the fairy lights and the glowing pool. It's fabulous."

They piled up their plates with grilled shrimp, salad and bread.

"It's my one indulgence," Lily said, pride in her voice for her backyard oasis.

"Your one?" Roxanna said.

Lily rolled her eyes. "Fine, I don't have a problem with indulgences."

"Did you have any idea about the shower?" Roxanna asked Miranda.

"None. In fact, I thought I was being the sneaky one."

"How so?" Lily asked.

Miranda looked at Lily, then at her soon-to-be mother-in-law, Katie. "By inviting Turner to come to dinner tonight with me and Cruz. A quiet little double date if you will. You've been drooling over him for days. Fireworks are ready to explode every time I've seen you together."

Lily's entire face blushed. Not exactly good manners to talk about the man she was drooling over in front of that man's mother. Katie had become a dear friend, and she couldn't do anything to jeopardize that friendship.

Katie started laughing. She got herself some shrimp then put her hand on Lily's cheek. "He couldn't find anyone better, dear."

Lily didn't say anything, but she didn't have to. Her friends grabbed onto the subject and sprinted.

"Speaking of indulgences" — Gabby sighed — "are you going to partake, Lily? Miranda's right about the fireworks. He could barely keep his smoldering eyes off you tonight. I thought we were going to have to put out a fire." Gabby batted her eyelashes and fanned her face with her hands.

Partake? She'd done more than partake. She'd, *they'd* already eaten each other alive. And she hadn't told a soul.

"He was smoldering at her, wasn't he?" Mary said and refilled everyone's cocktails. "Not to mention he made an appetizer to bring tonight. A chef — not a bad quality to have in the person who's interested in getting his hands all over you."

"Good Lord, Mama!" Gabby said, laughing.

"You started it, honey, and Katie knows how handsome her sons are." Mary winked at Katie. "Besides, it is a bridal shower, isn't it?"

"I will say," Miranda began, "Cruz makes the best cannelloni I've ever had, and his breakfasts are to die for. He certainly has skilled hands." Miranda blushed as Gabby and Mary dissolved into laughter.

Lily looked over at Roxanna, who was nursing Serafina. She didn't tease. Roxanna knew her secrets, her one true heartbreak, and knew what his return would mean.

"You okay?" Roxanna asked quietly.

"I've been avoiding you," Lily admitted.

"I wouldn't have left you alone to stew much longer."

"What?" Miranda said, looking between the two women. "I missed something, didn't I?"

"It's nothing," Lily said. "This is your night. We should be talking about you and the wedding and sexy lingerie."

"There you go changing the subject again, Lily. Tell us. We're your friends. You trust us."

It wasn't her friends she didn't trust. It was the words, saying them out loud. It was her heart she didn't trust. She'd tucked her love for Turner, the pain of his humiliating lecture when she was seventeen and the fact that he'd left all those years ago, into a tiny hidden part of her heart and now it was spilling out onto everything.

"Lily." Miranda put her hand on Lily's cheek. "Your expression is full of pain."

She covered her face. She never could hide her emotions. It had never bothered her before. She lived her life out in the open with vibrancy, grabbing at it, enjoying the hell out of it.

She let out a ragged breath and got up to walk around her deck. "Remember, Miranda, when I told you I'd been in love once before? It's Turner. I've been in love with him since I was a girl." She glanced at Katie, then covered her face with her hands. "God, this is embarrassing."

"I could see how much you cared for him when you were younger," Katie said. "I saw your pain when he left. And I love you like my own daughter. You are fabulous for him."

"Wow," Miranda said. "What happened? Why didn't you tell me? He's been back for weeks now. I'm an idiot. No wonder you've been acting weird, storming around, muttering to yourself. I've been too caught up in Cruz and the wedding and everything else. It didn't even occur to me that something was wrong. I'm so sorry, Lily."

"I was pretending he didn't affect me." She sat, unable to find peace standing or sitting. "Obviously, I wasn't doing a very good job, but if you had asked me earlier, I might have snapped your head off. I'm a mess.

I don't know what to do, and I always know what to do."

"Gabby's right. He couldn't take his eyes off you tonight," Roxanna offered. "Does he know how you feel?"

"God no! Are you kidding me? He'd die from laughter at the fact I've nursed a crush for over twelve years. He already thinks me foolish, temperamental. And it's not like he's here to stay. Having him walk away when we were kids was one thing, but to fall in love with him all over again, only to have him leave once more? There's no way I'll let him take with him the knowledge that I love him."

"Maybe he's not leaving again." Miranda took her hand. "And I don't get the impression he thinks you're foolish in the least. Every time I talk to him about your designs for Brockman House, he's very interested and he praises your work. He's even been out there helping build the dang thing. He believes in you."

Lily was stunned to hear all that. She'd been so busy being both annoyed and obsessed with him that she hadn't paid attention to what he'd been doing since he'd returned. Or rather, what it all meant. His interest in the hardware store, his concern over her father, jumping in and helping his brothers around the farm. Leaving little gifts for her. She wanted to hope, but it was too difficult, too painful to hope for something she knew would never be hers. Believing in her skill and liking her designs weren't enough.

"It doesn't matter," Lily said. "No offense, Katie, but he's irritating. His ego is bigger than this state. And he's…he's so bossy."

She looked at the stunned looks on her friends' faces right before they all burst out laughing. Not just a little laughter—they hooted at her. Miranda wiped tears from her eyes. Roxanna tried to burp Serafina while simultaneously laughing. Gabby and Mary juggled the plates on their laps. And Katie just smiled at her.

"Bossy?" Roxanna raised an eyebrow. She handed baby Serafina to Lily and made a plate of food for herself. "You're bossy as hell." She said the last word on a whisper, quickly glancing at Ana in the pool.

"You *are* the bossiest person I know, Lily," Gabby said, tenderness in her voice. "You two should be perfect for each other."

"It obviously *does* matter. You haven't been acting like yourself since he came home," Miranda said.

"Here, love," Gabby said, reaching out to Lily. "Let me take Serafina so you can open some wine since we finished your amazing daiquiris."

"How do you know his plans, whether he's staying or going? Have you asked him?" Mary said.

"I'm too afraid," she admitted and felt the tears sting her eyes. "I'm a coward." No way in hell was she going to tell them all how she'd run away from him after they'd made love on the kitchen counter in the cottage. She hated acting like a chicken, let alone admitting it.

"You are not a coward," Roxanna said. "You are one of the strongest women I've ever known. You've proven yourself extremely talented in a physically demanding profession. You weathered your mother's death when you were a girl. You've traveled the world solo, unafraid to try to adventure. You came home to care for your father and start your own business. You build things with your bare hands, Lily. I'm not friends with cowards. Only strong, vibrant women."

"Talk about bossy." Lily smiled at Roxanna, and all the amazing women surrounding her.

"It's true, no one here on this deck is a coward, least of all you, Lily," Katie said. "Let that sink into your beautiful head. And let's figure out what to do about the handsome son of mine who couldn't keep his eyes off you earlier tonight. If girlfriends can't help you with problems of the heart, then we're no good. And wouldn't I love to have him make his home here in Graciella, finally."

"And," said Miranda, "I can't think of a better place to talk about the heart than a bridal shower."

* * * *

They finished dinner and devoured the chocolate mousse before they tucked Ana in on the couch to watch a movie and the ladies returned to the deck to sip Spanish coffees and champagne and open presents.

Lily held a sleeping Serafina again, loving the warmth of the tiny head nuzzled on her shoulder, while Roxanna wrote down Miranda's gifts. There was lots of lingerie, a collection of love poems, a basket full of delicious-looking cookbooks and euros for their honeymoon to Europe in the fall. Miranda was opening Lily's first gift. A black-and-white photograph from an evening a few weeks ago of Cruz and Miranda standing out by the far horse pasture. They were in each other's arms, lost in each other's eyes. Lily had blurred the edges to take advantage of that ethereal late-afternoon light.

Gabby peered over Miranda's shoulder and handed her tissues. "It's so beautiful. It captures you and Cruz in love perfectly. It's dreamy. If I wasn't so happy for you, I'd be insanely jealous."

Sara Ohlin

"I'm so lucky," Miranda said. She passed the framed photo to Roxanna and went to kiss Lily's cheek.

"Cruz isn't the only one who knows how to use a camera," Lily said.

"It's perfect. Thank you."

"You have one last present, Miranda."

Lily winked at her. "I couldn't resist. I knew the picture would make you cry. The last gift should make you blush."

Miranda opened a red box. From the dark tissue paper, she lifted a black lace negligee made of a sexy but romantic floral pattern that wouldn't hide much of her skin but would most definitely have Cruz on his knees worshiping her body. Miranda's pale skin did indeed turn rosy. But she smiled too. The smile of a woman who was madly in love with a hottie who would be her husband at the end of summer.

"It is the most beautiful thing I've ever seen. I love it." Miranda raised her glass of champagne. "I couldn't ask for anything more, coming here to Graciella. I found love and something else that had been missing from my life for so long, precious, beautiful friends and family. I love you all."

"To you and Cruz, my friend. To every happiness you ever dreamed about," Lily said.

Gabby poured more champagne and they toasted and giggled surrounded by the stars.

"It's a good thing none of us has to drive ourselves home," Gabby said.

"Thank goodness for the men." Katie raised her glass.

"I bet they're not having as much fun as we are," Roxanna said, and they all tumbled into laughter again.

"Better them than us," Mary said. "With four of your little ones at home plus my three teenage girls to drive them crazy, whew! I almost feel like we owe them a night out. Almost."

Chapter Eighteen

The living room in Miguel and Roxanna's house looked like a tornado had blown through, somehow leaving all the walls intact but tossing toys, books, craft supplies, goldfish crackers, plastic cups and popcorn everywhere. Adam was flat on his back. Miguel's boys, Jose and Juan Carlos, were building a Lego bridge over his stomach. *There must be a million Legos strewn all over this house.*

Wearing one of Roxanna's aprons, Cruz swept up the destruction on the kitchen floor with help from the chocolate lab, Donut, who lapped the spilled soda. Miguel walked downstairs from putting Alicia and Bianca to bed, plopped himself face down on one of the couches and, without even looking, pointed the remote toward the television and turned off the princess movie.

Mary's three teenage girls had finally stopped drooling over Adam, Cruz and Turner, and had hidden themselves away in the guest room they were sharing.

Turner could hear giggling over their pop music. He tried to put the kids' books back in some semblance of order on the bookshelf by the television cabinet.

"Leave it, Turner," Miguel said. "There's no hope. You put them all back. Then poof! You turn around and they're all over the place again. Some invisible explosion happens every day. Multiple times a day. I swear, my nights off from the restaurant are one million times more chaotic than a kitchen rush."

"Beer?" Cruz asked. He passed out a bottle to each of the men. "I think we earned it."

Miguel raised his head. "Don't tell anyone if I start crying, okay? I'm trusting you men to keep it between us. They're children. I should be able to handle *children*," Miguel whined.

"*I'm* crying for you." Turner sank into one of the recliners and leaned the cold beer bottle on his forehead. "I feel like we fought a battle and lost with heavy casualties."

"We did." Miguel's muffled voice came from the couch cushion. "You ready for this, Cruz? Marriage, kids, destruction of property? Loss of every brain cell? There's still time to walk away and save yourself, you know."

Cruz laughed and tossed his apron into the laundry room. "No walking away for me, pal, but I'll admit, I don't think anyone's ever ready for six kids."

"How do you do this every day?" Turner asked.

"I'm insane." Miguel sat up. "How do you think I do it? Roxanna. That's how. She's the general around here, my general and my angel." Miguel smiled when he said her name. Even with him looking like he'd been buried under rubble for days, anyone could tell the man was insanely happy, insanely in love.

"I'm having fun." Adam tickled Miguel's boys.

"Shut up before I pour my beer on you," Miguel said. "Tell me it's time to get the women? Think you can handle yourself, Adam, if we go pick up the ladies?"

"With pleasure." Adam handed his beer to Cruz, busted through the Legos and, grabbing one boy with each arm, lifted them like they weighed nothing. "To bed, young men, or I'll tickle you to death." Carrying one over each shoulder, he marched upstairs.

"Uncle Adam! You destroyed our bridge!"

"Shh, men, or you'll wake your sisters. We'll build it again. I promise. And next week we'll build another massive fort in the hayloft," Adam said.

"And no girls allowed!" Juan Carlos said.

"Of course, no silly girls allowed. Now remember, shh, or you'll wake your sisters and your mama will be angry with me."

"Bastard," Miguel said. "He's the best damn babysitter we've ever had. And he never looks the worse for wear. They actually *listen* to him."

"Come on, friend. I'm ready to find my beautiful fiancée and you need your general," Cruz said, patting Miguel on the back. "And who knows." Cruz grinned. "Maybe Turner will find who he's looking for too."

"Better fill me in. The very, very few brain cells I have left are now awake and curious." Miguel dragged himself up.

"Turner's drooling over Lily," Cruz said.

Miguel's smile was huge. Then he laughed so hard he looked like he might start crying.

"What the hell is so funny?" Turner asked.

"You." Miguel practically wheezed. "You have no idea what you're in for, man. She might chew you up and spit you out."

"Yeah." Turner smiled with mischief in his eyes. "She keeps trying. But I plan to wear her down. Let's just say she has no idea what she's in for."

Miguel sobered up and stared at Turner. "I think you, Turner Brockman, have no idea what you're in for. Liliana Moreno does not suffer fools."

"Guess I'd better act like the genius I am, then."

* * * *

Although he was exhausted from the evening with a handful of little ones and three nieces holding court, Turner actually had fun. Miguel and Roxanna's house was full of noise and life, warmth and color—everything missing from Turner's life. After reading a gazillion picture books and eating a crazy dinner, Alicia and Bianca had pulled him down to the couch and climbed onto his lap to snuggle while their movie played. It was obvious when they got to Lily's house that the ladies had had a much more relaxing evening than the men.

They sat on the back patio which shimmered under the dark sky. Sparkling party lights, a warm red glow from outdoor heaters and wavy pool water eclipsed them. Laughter and giddiness emanated. His found Lily resting in one of her cushiony patio chairs with the baby asleep on her shoulder. She saw him step onto the porch and locked onto his eyes. No smile, but no frown either. Just one long, intense study, searching, looking for answers. He wished he knew the questions she asked.

"You ladies have a good time?" Cruz leaned down to kiss Miranda.

"It was wonderful." Miranda glowed under the lights. "I can't believe you all planned this especially for me. Let's get married tonight, Cruz. Wait till you see the sexy lingerie I got. Oops, I'm supposed to wait till our wedding to show you."

"You're awful cute when you're tipsy," Cruz said. He pulled her close into his body.

Turner longed for that kind of intimacy, that trust. He felt his gaze swing back to Lily. She'd kept her powerful eyes on him. When at some point in his life he'd have ignored a look like that. Right now, it felt exactly right. Like she was nectar guiding him toward her and he wanted nothing more than to go wherever she led. He wondered if she knew the power she had over him.

That should scare him more than anything, letting someone else have power over him. Somehow his entire world and emotions had been turned upside down. Lily could have all the power she wanted. If she'd pull down her walls and trust him, he'd show her he would cherish that trust.

He reached out to gently take the sleeping infant, transferring the baby to his own shoulder, then held out his free hand to help her up. Surprise registered in her eyes. It made them vulnerable. Sparkly light glinted off them. There was something about surprising her that he was coming to find extremely appealing.

"I'll take her." Lily reached for the baby.

Turner pulled away. "I just spent the evening with four of her siblings hanging all over me. One seems like a piece of cake."

"Isn't she precious?" Katie nuzzled the baby. She squeezed Turner's hand then caught Lily into a hug. "Javier's here to get me. Goodnight, dear. This was wonderful."

"Turner." Miguel smacked him gently on the back. "You're a natural with kids. Who knew? Here, I'll put my sleeping beauty in her car seat."

"Looks like your party was a success," Turner said. "Lily?"

"I… You… I'm going to help everyone out." And she rushed away.

"Turner, that pâté was to die for." Gabby winked at him. "Come on, Mama, let's get Ana."

Turner gave Miranda a hug and piled gifts into Cruz's truck. While everyone was saying their goodbyes, he wandered back to the deck and started carrying empty bottles and glasses into the kitchen. There was music on, a stunning violin piece that he didn't recognize but made him think of haunting tears falling. Now in the stillness of the night, the aching music revved him up again. There was a need inside him, burning for what was to come, for Lily, for her touch. He wanted to be worthy of her.

Chapter Nineteen

She studied him, his back to her. He carefully washed champagne glasses at her sink, standing in her kitchen like he belonged there, barefoot and comfortable. The man was confusing the hell out of her. He'd spent hours with his brothers and Miguel taking care of four little kids and three moody teenagers. And seeing him with that tiny baby in his arms. The way his eyes always, *always* found Lily's and locked on.

Frozen, she felt absolutely frozen with what to do. In the cottage, they'd consumed each other. Had it only been a week ago? It had to be more because her world felt tilted. A world couldn't fall off its axis in one week, could it? Perhaps, if hearts were involved. Hers was. He'd been stealing parts of it for weeks. She'd realized it there on the floor, the sun setting beyond them when he worshiped her body. So she'd choked and escaped. Although escaped hardly seemed like the right word. She'd fled, but there'd been no freedom, no relief, no lightness for her this week. Only a storm of emotions battling inside her. Hope, turmoil, fear, love.

And now he was in her house, doing her dishes, waiting for her. He might have come tonight intent on having her, but he would let her make the decision. Here, at this moment she had to decide, because she only had so many pieces of her precious heart left. And she'd never been so frazzled over a decision in her life. She walked out to the deck and stood over the pool, hoping the mesmerizing glimmer of blue lights could guide her.

"The pool is lovely, Lily." He was there, so close, behind her.

The pool? Who wants to talk about the pool?

"Almost as lovely as you," he whispered. His hands settled on her shoulders. He drew circles on her neck with his thumbs and brought his lips close, so close without touching. "Are you my enchantress, come to make me yours? Your skin glows in the light." He kissed her then. One breathless kiss on her neck while he ran his hands through her curls to her scalp, kneading, relaxing her even as he made her entire body shiver with want. He traced a path up her neck to her ear. "Are you on fire for me, Lily? Or are you always like this, burning with desire?"

"No," she whispered, blinking away the tears at how precious he made her feel, how alive.

"No, what?" He nipped her earlobe.

"I've never felt like this before," she said, turning in his arms. The moment he whispered her name, she hadn't had a choice. She placed a hand on his cheek and on his chest where the buttons of his shirt were open. How long had she waited to feel the strength, the warmth of him? How long? And now she couldn't get enough. Now her caress spoke the words she couldn't get out. *Yes, Turner, make me yours.*

Turner captured her mouth with his. Caressing her shoulders, he pulled her into him and urged the kiss deeper.

All he had to do was stand close to her without touching and it felt like his body seared into hers, melting her nerves, making her forget all her worries. With his touch, she lost all reason. All she could focus on was how badly she wanted him. How her heart ached for him to want her. With his touch, he mesmerized.

"I've been wondering all night," he said, razing his eyes down her entire body.

"What?" she asked, her voice barely a whisper.

He took the straps of her dress in each of his hands. "Ever since I've gotten a look at all those lacy things that you wear under your unassuming work clothes, your black lace bra, and the pink one from the other evening." He paused and raised an eyebrow at her. "I've been wondering..." Ever so slowly, he dragged the straps off her shoulders and, with one tug, pooled the dress around her feet. He gulped. "What sexy piece you had on underneath this dress."

How smooth he was, but he couldn't hide the lust blazing in his eyes at seeing her completely naked.

"And?" She grew bolder. "Do you like what I have on underneath?"

He answered with one soft stroke up her body from her belly to her neck, to her lips. She quivered everywhere from that soft, confident caress and the way he looked at her.

"God, Turner." She'd lost herself. "Do that again, please."

His gaze followed the path of his fingers that stroked from her thighs, slowly up her belly, teasing over her nipples, then again to her lips.

"Magnificent," he growled before he fused his mouth with hers.

She wrapped her arms around him and fitted her entire body against his. Lost in his kiss, in the feelings that swamped through her. "My bedroom." She rasped out the words, not wanting his lips to leave hers even for a second.

"No." He drew lines over her lips with his tongue, tasting her. She needed so much more.

"Outside, under the stars and the lights, Lily. That's where I want to take you this time. To show you how stunning you are. You belong in this beauty."

Oh, his words tantalized and his tongue seduced.

He walked them both over to the double chaise. She'd gotten his shirt pushed down over his shoulders, but she gave up on his clothes and held on to him. Held on for life over the assault of his body razing over her naked skin with each step he took. He was like a furnace to her chilly skin, eliciting pinprick sensations like a million tiny shocks, tiny beautiful shocks full of pleasure.

They reached the chaise and so, so gently he laid her down on the cushion. He trailed feather-light touches over her breasts, to the insides of her thighs. And the man kept going all the way to her feet, backing up till he was standing again. Was he going to leave her there in this place of torture? He shrugged off his clothes, then put his full attention back on her. A soft breeze skipped over her skin, tangling with the warmth from the heaters, the lust in his eyes, and mimicked the way she felt inside—breathy, skittish, excited. A multitude of sensations blooming.

God, she wanted him on her. Instead of covering her and dragging her along for the ride, he removed her heels, placing a kiss on each foot. Then he moved to her legs, where he teased his lips up her inner thigh, while whispering words of adoration before he moved to the other leg. Worshiping every inch of her. He caressed. He kissed. He savored.

"Turner, I want you."

He smiled. "Thank God." His voice was unsteady. "I thought I was going to have to beg for you to say it again. Do you know what I want? To make you feel amazing, Lily. To make you feel how much I desire you. How I can't think about anything else except you."

He propped himself next to her on one hand and with the other, he traced a path between her breasts.

"Stunning, Lily. Your body, so beautiful, like a sculpture from an artist." While she was floating on the wave, he took as much as he gave, teasing, caressing. She sucked in her breath at the pleasure that raced through her, hot and heavy. Then he captured her skin with that sensual mouth of his, sucking, tasting, easing the bite of pain, the pain that had tuned her entire body in to pleasure.

She was high, barely aware of anything else at all except his hands and lips on her body, warm and soft, rough at times. A heady dream, this sensual person turning her body into an erotic dance. She lost herself in the image of Turner worshiping her skin, of flames leaping.

As he moved down her body, tasting, kissing, she lost all sense of time. All thoughts were replaced by the feeling of him. How magnificently he held her. Strong, confident hands searing her skin. He made love to her with his tongue, lifting her higher and higher. "Please," she breathed and came apart in his arms. And thank God he wasn't finished. She soared on her high and Turner stole back up the length of her body, slid a condom on in one swift move and entered her. She rose to meet him, gripping the chaise with the force of him.

"Open your eyes, Lily," Turner said. "Open your eyes and look at me. I love the way your eyes burn when they're full of passion."

She let go of the dream-like pictures his touch created in her mind, and met his eyes. The stormy gray green, the power, the intensity allowed her to be nowhere but here with him. And they rose together, exploding when their fires met, two souls waiting to be together.

Turner lay on top of her. He nuzzled into her neck and breathed in her scent now mixed with their lovemaking. He felt shocked to his core. He'd been electrocuted and was now left floating, completely ungrounded. Lily loosened her grip around his body and drew circles up and down his back.

"That feels amazing. You stun me, Liliana Moreno."

Shivers raced over her body at his words.

"Save anything wonderful you might say about me. I'm processing the tingling in my skin," she said.

Turner slid off and lay by her side. Her curves were soft and expressive at the same time. They held nothing back. Her skin was a treasure hunt he wanted to conquer, silky smooth, drawing him in. He was getting aroused again. Turner stood, picked her up and said, "Now you can tell me where your bedroom is."

"Put me down, Turner. I can find my bedroom by myself. You're free to leave if you want."

She'd stiffened when he picked her up, shivered. With fear? With longing? The heat between them now turned to a cold layer of sweat. But he could see into her panic. She'd let it go enough to make love, but now, in the aftermath, she was all nerves again. What would it take to convince this woman? He would ignore her attempt at dismissal. She could put up her walls and he would keep knocking them down. "Who said anything about leaving? I enjoy practicing conversations with you. Where's your bedroom, Lily? I want to take you there so you can rock my world all over again."

She stared at him, hesitating only a moment, then she put her hand on his cheek. "Down the hall," she answered, never taking her eyes from his.

Chapter Twenty

Rock his world she did. Too bad he didn't get to linger in those feelings the next morning. Even before he got out of bed and searched her house, Turner knew she was gone. The absence of her was powerful in its own way. Everything around her hummed with life when she was near. Now, her house rested, too quiet, asleep until her return. He was alone.

No goodbye kiss or "Last night was great." He walked out to her front porch to find her truck gone. Actually, if she'd said their night was great, he would have murdered her, because last night had been earth-shattering. His body was still nearly wiped out, but his mind raced. Well, they'd established that she was good at running. And now *he* was starting to get pissed.

The damn woman did not strike him as a coward, someone who hid from their fears, but she acted like a scared kitten around him whenever they got close. He was angry, but more than that he was confused. What in the hell about him, about the two of them together had her so afraid she'd run every time? He wanted to court her, to be with her, to maybe, hopefully, build a life with her. All things he thought aligned with her desires. *Well, fuck, maybe she just doesn't want it all with you.*

He still wanted to know the story behind her being pissed at him, and he knew there was a story. Now he also wanted to know what scared her so much that she sought escape. Were the two connected? Had he done something to her in the past to make her angry and to make her so afraid of getting close to him? He needed answers and he'd be damned if he'd wait till the next time she felt like letting him into her bed, then acting like it was no big deal. He wanted a relationship with her and there was no way in hell they could have that if she wasn't being honest with him and with herself.

A rush of awareness surged through him at the thought that he'd been living that exact same way since he had left Graciella twelve years ago. Realization was a swift kick to his gut. He never wanted to live that way again, closed off and scared. And he certainly didn't intend for the woman he was in love with and planned to spend the rest of his life with to live that way either.

The drive to the theater did nothing to stem Turner's temper. If anything it gave him more time to simmer. He was near to boiling when he pulled up next to her truck.

She was sitting on the floor, painting the baseboards in the lobby. Tina Turner's voice blasted from the speakers, and Lily was smiling, but it wasn't a smile of happiness. It was like she was lost, swept up in a sadness he couldn't understand. Her beauty caught him off guard. It was staggering to see into the heart of her, the way she felt emotions so deeply and the way they echoed back out of her for all the world to see. And she put those emotions into everything — building, cooking, the music she played, when she made love. Why would she try to keep something so brilliant from being free? Why did she run?

More than many, he knew fear, and he knew how to hide from it, how to bury it in work, in his career. Which meant he also knew how unfulfilled the running and hiding left him. How a person could never bury it deep enough. It was always there, lingering, a dingy residue he couldn't scrape off. God, how he could see his own actions reflected so clearly in hers now. And he felt like the biggest idiot on the planet.

The most fulfilled he'd felt in the last ten years was since being back here in Graciella, working with his brothers, imagining an amended career, being with Lily, fighting with her, seducing her, making love to her. All of this because he'd finally let his heart feel again. He'd risked vulnerability, knowing there could be pain, but oh how much love and pleasure there was too. He didn't know how to make her see that he would cherish her heart, if she'd let him. And he'd give her his — he already had.

Then she opened her mouth and her words ignited his anger once more.

"Didn't get enough of me last night, Turner?" She tried to infuse her words with a lazy, unconcerned edge. She'd heard him walk in and ignored him. Had heard the door shut behind him and hoped she could still her rapidly beating heart and pretend he didn't affect her that much. He'd followed her to the theater, and she knew he'd ravish her again. And she was glad. It was what she wanted. *Isn't it?* Ever since he'd touched her, she couldn't assuage this edgy need she had for him. So he'd take her quick and hungry, then she could get back to work. Try to bandage her heart for how much it hurt to love him knowing he could never be hers. She'd watched him sleep this morning, ached to touch him, to fit her body to his and stay safe in his arms, but his arms weren't for her and instead she'd nearly been sick at that thought. If she felt this unsteady already, how would she deal with her shattered heart when he left? Maybe she never should have started this madness. Maybe she should wish for him to leave now and never touch her again.

"What the hell is wrong with you?" He grabbed the brush out of her hands, dropped it in the paint tray and hauled her to her feet. Then he let her go and paced back and forth, a simmering pot of pissed off, or hurt? "Why do you keep doing that?" he seethed.

She felt the loss of his touch like a wound. "Doing what?" She was shaking inside, and it was all she could do not to let him see. But it wasn't fear of him — the fear was of her heart, how deeply already she felt for him again.

"Leaving, dammit! Walking away from me, from this thing that's between us? We just had one of the most incredible nights together and I wake up and you're gone. Without a word, a note, a kiss. Every time we've connected, you can't handle it and you walk away. Actually, you don't walk, you flat out run scared."

"I...I don't know," she said. Her voice sounded weak. God, how she hated that feeling. Experiencing it was one thing, letting him witness it made her sick.

"You do know. You just won't tell me. You're afraid of something, and you keep punishing me for something I didn't do, or something I did that I don't know about. What is it, Lily?"

"It's nothing, Turner." She turned away and sucked in a few deep breaths. "Why do you care anyway? You're only here for a quick visit. You don't want this life in Graciella. I don't owe you anything."

"How in the hell do you know what I want? All these things you think you know are assumptions you've dreamed up. Have I once given you any indication I wanted a quick fuck and then see ya? You're the one treating it like that, not me." She flinched at the harsh angry tone to his voice. *Is he right? Is that how I'm treating him?* She'd seen it as protecting herself. Never once had she meant to demean him.

There was no way he'd want to stay here. Want all of her—stubborn, obsessed with work, untidy. Would he? No way, and he was *angry* with her when he was the one who blew in from his fancy life and would leave them all in smithereens when he blew back out. No, Lily did not like being called an idiot when the real idiot was standing right in front of her.

"You haven't given me any indication of anything else," she yelled back.

"Bullshit! Somehow you have that notion in your head, but I did nothing to put it there. And communication isn't exactly your strong suit, is it? You don't stick around long enough to ask me anything. Or you ask then take off before I can answer. You let yourself get close to me physically, but when it's over, you completely shut me out with anger. Try having a conversation. You could start by telling me why you're so pissed at me. Why me, Lily?"

"Okay, damn you, you left!" she yelled. She didn't like being backed into a corner. Fine, he wanted the truth. He could have it. Maybe if she finally gave it to him, she wouldn't feel the weight of it dragging her down, following her everywhere. "You left without ever saying goodbye all those years ago. But before that you hurt me. And I don't know what's worse, that you hurt me or that you don't even remember doing it." She watched the confusion take over his face, easing some of the lingering temper in his eyes.

"Tell me what I did. I don't remember and I can't apologize or understand unless you explain it to me."

She roamed the suddenly too small theater lobby, feeling like a caged lion. Her heart wanted to jump out of her body. Love, anger, fear, regret, want — all these emotions banged around inside her, wearing her down. She didn't know what the hell to do with any of them. How to order them, control them.

"Lily, please," he begged, his voice softer.

"Junior year, well, senior year for you, I was walking home from school one day when one of the football players started harassing me. It was…scary. He freaked me out. It could have gotten bad, I think." She sucked in a deep breath. All this time she'd locked that moment of fear away deeper than all the rest. That black moment when she'd truly been scared for her safety. "You came upon us, fought him off, and he ran. You saved me from something potentially awful happening." The words rushed out of her.

He stared at her and the memory slowly dawned.

"Christ," he swore softly. "I remember now. At least I remember the red rage inside me when I saw Will Brixton with his hands on you. But I'm confused. You're mad because I helped you?"

"Then," she said her voice hoarse with trying to hold back the emotion, "you treated me like the dirt on your shoe, lecturing me, yelling at me, like it was *my* fault, Turner. Like I was to blame for that jerk harassing me. And you insisted on walking me home after that. For a month you walked me home. But you never spoke to me, you never saw *me*, and..." *I was so in love with you.*

She couldn't tell him. She was mortified enough having to relive the entire incident. "You were so angry you had to *babysit* me. I never asked you to, but you did it anyway and I felt like shit every day because I just wanted you to talk to me, to see me."

He stared at her across the wide expanse that seemed now like an entire desert between them. And she turned away at the onslaught of his intense focus. His eyes were trying to break into the very core of her. She couldn't bear to be so exposed. He was right. She kept trying to close herself off to him emotionally.

"I... Lily," he said, letting out a deep breath. She felt him walk closer. She was so acutely aware of his presence.

"Lily." He gently took her hands and she let him, slumped out a sigh at his connection. He wrapped her arms around his body, pulled her head to him and pressed it against his chest and held her. She didn't speak, couldn't have managed to get words out, but she let his embrace relax her.

"I remember more now. I have no excuse, no way to apologize for yelling at you and making you feel that way and for not seeing you," Turner said. "I was near blind with disgust when I saw him trying to kiss you and you shoving at him. All I could think was that was how T.D. treated women. And T.D. wanted me to emulate him. I let my anger take over. I let it take over when I walked you home that day and every day after. I was consumed with disgust for T.D. and I hated myself for never being able to protect the people around me. And…at one point for wanting T.D.'s love.

"I was a young, confused, egotistical kid with a huge chip on his shoulder. It wasn't that I didn't see *you*, Lily. I could barely see past my own anger and shame. I was crawling out of my skin with the need to get out of Graciella. God, I was a piece of work. It was one thing to hate T.D. Easy to do since he was such a horrible excuse for a human. But…I…to have loved someone like that? It's…it feels even worse than the hate. How could I have ever loved him? How could I have *wanted* his love? The shame was overwhelming. When it finally occurred to me that he was grooming me to act like him, well…"

Even though he held her, he felt so far away, lost in his own pain. Everything he said made so much sense. She'd only ever seen his rejection of her, because she'd been head-over-heels in love with him. How stupid not to realize what he must have been going through. She'd been just like Turner, barely seeing past anything but her own emotions. His arms latched tighter, as though even if she tried to escape, he wouldn't let her. Or maybe he took comfort in her arms too. Could she care for him? She'd never once thought of that, what *she* could give him, what his needs were too. Lily gripped him in her own fierce hug.

"Turner." She reached a hand up to his cheek. "I'm so sorry. Of course you wanted his love. You were his son. You were a child." Now she was furious for him. How much he must have struggled all this time with a shame that wasn't his to own. "We *all* want our parents' love. Especially someone like you who is so full of life and love himself. Every single child wants that, deserves that. And you have to know, you are nothing like that man."

"I look like him. I became a shrewd businessman. I have his DNA."

Ugh, his emotions bled out of him, breaking her heart. "His blood does not make you like him in any important way. A man can be smart in business without being mean and committing crimes. And when I look at you, Turner, the handsomest man I've ever seen, your beauty stuns me because of the kind of man you are—honest, loving, passionate, silly, strong, stubborn, caring—not because of your misty green eyes or rumbly voice. Or hot body."

He chuckled as she'd hoped he'd do. "Misty green eyes?"

"Yes, Turner. I can't help it. I get lost in them. They remind me of the fog on chilly morning. But do you get what I'm saying? You are not that cruel man. You are the opposite. You take care of the people you love."

"It's hard to hear that last part and not feel guilt for all the years I stayed away and tried to shove this place from my memories." She'd been part of that layer of guilt.

"I'm sorry if I added to that. Me and my huffiness. You were trying to escape your shame and the wounds from an entire childhood. You were surviving the best way you knew how."

Turner buried his head in her neck. "Helps to be here with you, to get it out. Still doesn't make up for me being a jackass all those years ago. I'm sorry for hurting you, Lily." His tender voice soothed her heart. No, he was nothing like T.D. Brockman.

"If you were an ignorant, egotistical kid, I was a naive and stupid teenager. A girl with a silly crush. I never even thought about how T.D.'s treatment made you feel."

"It feels like time to quit giving T.D. power over us."

"Yes," she sighed.

He looked at her then, his smile replacing the haunted look. "You had a crush on me? Is that something else I can't remember? Another piece to this puzzle of you I'm trying to put together? Boy, I was more of an idiot than I thought." He kept his arms around her and walked her slowly back up against the wall, pinning her gently with his body.

God, but she loved how his body felt against hers. Warm, strong, open, wanting. His arousal hard and tight against her.

"I see you now, Lily. I see you," he said. One hand rubbed up and down her back. She arched with that sweet stroke, basking in his attention. She was lost in his touch.

"You know I'm still just an egotistical kid." His voice had deepened the way it did when he wanted to devour her. She wasn't sure which was more arousing, his voice or his body, both speaking a secret language to her of desire, of need. To be wanted by Turner Brockman was a childhood wish come true. To be needed by him was her heart's deepest desire.

"Tell me again about this crush." He kissed her chin, her cheeks and her eyebrows. Taking care. "Beautiful Lily had a crush on me," he whispered, his soft lips tickling her ear. She felt him smile against her skin. It sent fireworks through her. "I think you still have a crush on me."

Now her body was overwhelmed, assaulted by his tenderness. "Turner," she said on a breathless sigh. He teased down her neck, kneaded his fingers into her hips, holding her against the wall even while she tried to arch close to him and every part of her opening.

"I definitely have a crush on *you*, Lily." Without wasting a moment, he snaked one hand up under her shirt, teasing, so slowly, exploring her skin. Seducing with his hands as well as his mouth. Starving, like her. Her need for him felt explosive.

With each breath he took, he called her name, "Lily, Lily, Lily," caressing her heart with his words. "I have a crush on your sharp mind."

"You do?" She was barely able to find her breath.

She closed her eyes to the sensations he elicited. Her breasts heavy with want, she heard moaning and realized it was her own.

"A crush on your skin." He took his hands away, but before she could complain, he unbuttoned her shirt and started the same teasing dance with his tongue and lips and kisses on her chest. Each pass of his fingers, each taste, each scrape of his teeth on her breasts sent shocks streaking through her body.

"I have a crush on your temper." He nipped her skin through her bra and finally she could move into him, into the exquisite pain that immediately sent pleasure to her core. He soothed with a cool breath. "A crush on your curves, the way they fit in my hands." Mmm, he found his way into her jeans, around her hips and held her. Rough hands caressed her ass, while his mouth adored her chest. She didn't know whether to lean into that mouth or rub her soft flesh against his wicked hands. She felt like a wild animal fretting with uncoordinated movement, not wanting to lose the delicious feel of his intense glorious attention anywhere.

He laughed against her neck. "You like that. Good. I have a crush on making you feel amazing, Lily."

Fantastic, frantic. Needy. He made her feel everything. She moaned again when he gave her breasts little sharp nips of pleasure. She floated, lost herself to the high, hovered in some sensual place. He unzipped her jeans and traced every so lightly under the seam of her underwear.

"I most definitely have a crush on your body, Liliana." Slowly, tenderly he brushed his fingers along the sensitive flesh of her, as if he was caressing something precious the way he stroked, changing his tempo, watching her responses.

"There, Turner. Right there." But she didn't have to beg. He gave her everything. Holding her against him, he kissed her and dipped his fingers inside her core, while playing that perfect glorious spot with his thumb, like a musician with his instrument. She reared against the wall and lost herself in the shuddering thunder of her body coming apart under his touch. He kept her there, his mouth on hers, his fingers conducting her pleasure, until she had nothing left.

"So beautiful, so passionate, the way your body responds to my crush, Lily," Turner whispered in her ear. She rested her head on his shoulder. Still holding her, he fixed her clothes, then wrapped his arms around her keeping her against him while her body calmed from the finale. She was grateful he held her, because she wasn't sure she could stand on her own.

"There's something to be said for having crushes as adults," he said.

She giggled. "Oh, I don't know, my teenage crush on you was pretty epic."

"Tell me about it."

"Well, there was the cliché batting of eyelashes and exaggerated sighs every time you were near. Everything I said came out sounding stupid, so I remained quiet. Even though I hated riding bikes, I'd race with you and your brothers so you would notice me. Unfortunately, I always lagged behind. Stupid bike. I sat in the stands at all your track meets, your swim meets. I journaled about you," she said dramatically, and felt him laugh.

"More," he said. "Tell me everything. Did you circle my name with hearts and write Lily Brockman next to it?"

Then she laughed outright. "The hearts yes. The name no way. Moreno is my name forever."

"Good," he said and kissed her heart over her shirt again. She loved this, talking with him about silly childhood moments. They'd both had their share of trauma growing up and yet, there had still been so much beauty. Maybe even more for her she realized as she thought of boy Turner longing for a father's love, for a father to be worthy of his son's love. She could give him this, her own childhood fantasies, ridiculous though they were.

"I had our first date daydreamed in technicolor. You'd ask me out to the movies, here." She gestured around them. "You'd be nervous because you liked me so much. So you'd hold my hand, because you wanted to and because it made you feel steady. You'd buy the biggest popcorn for us to share and chocolate too. There was always going to be chocolate. Oh! Or maybe donut holes. Oh my gosh, I have got to get a donut machine for the theater." He chuckled into her and squeezed her own laugh out. "I'd get to sit next to you in the dark. In my favorite place with my favorite person while magic happened on screen. And when the movie started and you were captivated, I'd watch you and memorize the moment." Lost in her silly memory, it both broke her heart and healed it a bit. Not so silly, dreams of a young girl, because she could picture that special image today. A first date with Turner Brockman, no longer a boy, but maybe he'd still want, *need* to hold her hand.

The silence brought her back to reality. "Turner." She nudged him and he opened his eyes.

"Sorry, I was enjoying the picture you painted. I'd have to amend it, though because I'd be hoping to kiss you in the dark, not watching the screen. I'd be so nervous I'd have no idea what movie was playing. But I'd be with you, which is everything. I like imagining this with you." He twirled her around into the sunlight filtering across the floor. "Come with me tonight, Lily. They're having another big outdoor dinner tonight at the farm, practicing for the farm-to-table dinners. Join me?" He smiled and nipped at her bottom lip. "You have the most sensual gorgeous eyes, like fire. I have a crush on those eyes too. Come with me to dinner."

"You say things, Turner. Such lovely things, and I don't have any defense against your beautiful words." She took a deep breath at the admission. "I'd love to."

He tilted her face up to look at him. "You make me feel, Lily. You make me say things I haven't ever said to another person. Your passion shimmers all over and when you share it with me, it humbles me. But you look serious and sad. Why?"

She shook her head. She was completely exposed and open to him and it scared the hell out of her. "Not sad. Touched, Turner. I'd love to come to the dinner tonight. I need to finish some painting, but I'll come over to the farm later."

"How about I pick you up at your house and drive us over together," Turner said.

"Really, Turner, there's no need."

"Lily." He shook her gently. "No more hiding from me, not after everything we just shared. Not after how vulnerable we just were with each other."

"You're right, I'm sorry. It's my automatic, I think, to push away, to make space."

He studied her. "If I pick you up, then I get to drive you home and you can invite me to spend the night again. You asked me what I wanted. The answer is you. I want to spend the night with you. Then I want to wake up *together*, make breakfast and kiss you before you leave for work in the morning. I want to be with you. What you need to ask yourself, Lily, the woman you are now, is what does *she* want. Think about that during your day. Think about me." He kissed her one last gentle time. And still it knocked the earth out from under her.

As if she ever stopped thinking about him. *I want you too*, she wanted to cry. *I've always wanted you, but I'm too afraid to tell you.* How easy it was to chat about wishes from childhood, exaggerated, silly, foolish. Except they weren't to her, any of those things. She wanted all of those wishes — foolish though they may have been, *may be* — to come true. With him.

"I'll pick you up at six-thirty. Our first semi-date." He strolled backward out of the theater.

"Semi-date?"

"Until I can meet the standards of your beautifully imagined first date, I'm calling it a semi-date." Then he gave her a crooked grin. And she stood there staring and smiling long after he'd gone.

Chapter Twenty-One

Turner filled a large bin with ice, beer and bottles of white wine. Cruz stood next to him, grilling the pizzas. For a moment, Turner took in his surroundings. Miranda, Katie and Gabby were setting the long tables. Adam helped Javier string lights from the trees over the tables. Roxanna sat in a wicker rocker, cutting flowers for jam jars. A perfect, warm, summer night. No humidity. Quiet save for the happy noises of kids laughing and playing.

He sought out Lily. He liked seeing her with his family, *her family*. They'd always been hers too. Perhaps more so since she hadn't been the one to flee. *Ha!* At least not from his family. And hopefully no longer from him. He'd seen the sadness in her eyes at the theater. He'd made her sad *again*, even if she hadn't admitted it. While he'd never felt more free and loved and phenomenal in his life. Not only had he dug out why she kept putting up her walls, but in doing so he'd been able to shed some of his own burdens. She hadn't judged him. She'd embraced him, all of him, flaws and unreasonable child desires and crap bloodlines. And he didn't know if she realized it, but in sharing her young dreams of them together, not only had she given him a gift, but she'd opened herself completely to him. Now he had to guarantee he would keep her heart and all her vulnerabilities and dreams safe and treasured.

She didn't look sad now. She played soccer on the grass in bare feet with Miguel and a bunch of kids, some Miguel's, some belonging to the migrant farm workers. Her sundress danced around her knees. And she'd stuck a bunch of glittery barrettes in to tame her curls. Hmm, he loved how her neck was always accessible and how his lips felt right at home kissing that neck. Her cheeks were flushed, and she was laughing, a full deep laugh. Holding that gorgeous sound to his heart he felt that ache again. It was almost overwhelming. He reached up and rubbed at his chest.

"Turner Brockman alive and breathing. Never thought I'd see the day. It's good to see you, man. Where the hell have you been?"

"Jake Burns." Turner smiled and shook Jake's hand. "It's good to see you too. Wait a minute, that your law practice in town? Burns Law Practice?"

"It is. Need some representation?"

Turner laughed. "What in the hell is a good old boy from Harvard doing all the way out here in Graciella?"

"I blame it on you and Cruz. It's all you two talked about in college. Especially those summers we worked together for Griff's dad, framing house after house in the sweltering New England summers. Your descriptions and stories of this place kept me from losing it in that heat. The tall pine trees, the blue skies, the smell of the ocean breeze. I took a long road trip after law school, ended up in Portland and decided to stay."

"Jesus, I don't remember that," Turner said. He was stunned that he'd ever spoken of this place in a good way.

"You don't remember how miserable we were building houses in that sauna? Even though we got a view of the girls' field hockey team in August?"

"The heat and the girls I remember," Turner said with a grin. "Sharing fond memories of this place, I don't."

"Don't worry. You never got too sentimental. You mostly talked about the cool, cool breeze. I think you did it more to torture me while we sweated our guts out on those roofs. Overall you were a moody, quiet bastard. I won't say anything to ruin your reputation."

"So, you're a big bad lawyer now? Defending all manner of criminals," Turner said.

Jake laughed. "More like estate planning and settling wills, some financial law, real estate law. My head's stuck in a book or paperwork most days. I started my practice in Portland, but when Cruz came back, I rented a space in downtown. I'd like to buy some land here and build myself a house."

"Now you're the one getting sentimental," Turner teased.

"What about you? How long are you back for, Turner?"

"That's something we're all wondering." Cruz pinned Turner with a look.

"Oh, he's not going anywhere." Adam winked at Turner.

"How do you know?" Turner asked

"Well, if my powers of observation are correct, I'd guess you're head over heels in love with our Lily, or at least well on your way. An intelligent man like you wouldn't let an amazing woman go to move back to some lonely life in Berlin. You seem *happy* here."

Cruz started laughing, Jake had a huge grin on his face and Turner stood there, too stunned to say anything.

"It's written all over your face every time you look at her and talk about her. I may be the youngest, but I've always been the smartest."

Turner watched Lily. Ana and Jose tackled her onto the grass and started tickling her. He couldn't help his smile. "I'm a goner, but don't tell her that. You'll scare her halfway around the world. You'd think I'd be the one to take convincing that I could be happy here. After all the years I tried to shove this place from my mind. I am happy. I haven't been in a long time. I do want to stay. And I want her with me. But she's afraid of something and she won't tell me what it is."

Adam put his arm around Turner's shoulders. "Don't give up on her. If she thinks you're only here for a visit, it's not likely she'd let her guard down all the way. She's got a vulnerable heart. But I have faith in you."

Turner clinked his bottle to Adam's. "Wish me luck, men. This may be the hardest challenge I've faced yet." He put his beer down, poured Lily a glass of wine and went to interrupt her soccer game.

"Here." Turner held his hand down to Lily. "Let me help you up."

"Thank you," she said, her eyes intent on his. He kept her hand after she'd gotten up and pulled it behind her with his to tug her close to him.

"Welcome." He kissed her, savoring the feel of her soft full lips. Loved the way her eyes got hazy and shuttered when they kissed. He pulled his head away a few inches and watched the emotions play out over her face, surprise, desire, need, annoyance.

Her body tensed. "Turner, everyone will see."

"I know." He grinned at her. Damn if she wasn't predictable sometimes. She'd been quiet on the drive over and he'd barely put the truck in Park tonight when she'd jumped out and started toward the back yard before he'd even opened his own door. "Why does that bother you?"

"I… It doesn't. I… You make me feel all these things," she said and paused. He could almost see the battle in her to continue. He warmed when she did, instead of shutting him out this time.

"I'm a mess inside and afraid and uncertain. It's hard for me to figure it all out alone, or with you, let alone surrounded by all these people I love."

Stunned with her open admission and grateful she'd offered it, he held her steady. *I've got you*. How could he not have seen from the very first moment how deeply vulnerable this amazing woman was? Bold, stubborn, loud, gorgeous. She presented all those to the world fearlessly. But her precious heart was her essence. He wanted to cherish every bit of her. He had to find a way to make her trust him.

"I'm not trying to embarrass you. But I do enjoy kissing you. Thirsty?" He handed her the glass of wine. She blinked and looked down at his offering.

"You make me feel things too, Lily. Lots of things I'm interested in exploring. And let me be very clear when I say this to you, I'm not going anywhere. I know you expect me to leave any minute, but — "

"You have a life in Berlin."

"Shh." He put a finger on her lips. "Let me finish. That *was* my life. When I arrived I definitely only intended to stay a few days. I came to exorcise ghosts. Jesus, I was so scared of coming back. I couldn't even handle the flight without alcohol. Lots and lots of alcohol to calm the black panic I was experiencing. But then I got here. And I found I could breathe. Not only was T.D. gone, but my family welcomed me. I've been busy building and fixing things with my hands that I love." He tightened his hold. "And I found you."

"Dinner's ready!" Cruz yelled across the field.

Annoyed at the interruption but aware this wasn't the place to continue the conversation, he leaned his forehead on hers and said, "I didn't have a life in Berlin, Lily. I had an empty shell of an existence. Just a job. I'm here to stay and you're going to have to get used to me." Kissing her once, he walked his beauty to dinner, their hands connected.

Chapter Twenty-Two

"Damn, girl! You better start talking now," Gabby said in the Brockman House kitchen after dinner. The men were outside, roasting marshmallows around the fire pit with Miguel's kids. Miranda had suggested the women do the dishes so they could grill Lily.

"Seriously," Miranda said. "Last night he couldn't keep his eyes off you. Tonight you show up with him and he can't keep his *hands* off you. In front of family."

"Not to mention," Gabby said, "you're glowing. And the way you kept sneaking glances at him during dinner, even though he was right next to you. Mmm hmm!"

"That kiss on the grass was pretty swoony." Roxanna nudged her shoulder and loaded the dishwasher. "The way he was holding you to him." She sighed. "Like he'd never let you go."

She didn't want him to let her go. "He told me he's staying," Lily said quietly.

"He did?" Miranda gasped.

"You look freaked out. I am so confused, honey. That he wants to stay is great news. I'd think you'd be giving us all high fives, blasting music from the speakers, jumping up and down with excitement. Why do you look miserable?" Roxanna said.

"I'm afraid he doesn't mean any of it. That he's not leaving, the nice things he says about me, the way he treats me. It's not that I think he's lying, only that he'll soon realize this isn't the place for him, little old Graciella. You know the kind of life he has, the projects he's been working on in Berlin. Sleek, expensive development deals. The kind of deals that come with lots of esteem, money and a major high. Why would he give up all that for me, for this?" Lily said, drawing her hands around in front of her.

"Why wouldn't he, is more like it." Gabby smacked Lily on the head.

"Hey! You're supposed to be supporting me," Lily said.

"My friendship does not mean supporting you being an idiot," Gabby said. "It's not about his career, or Berlin vs. Graciella. It's about you, Lily."

"He's in love," Miranda said, matter of fact.

"What?" Lily said.

"I think she's right, Lily," Roxanna said, smiling.

"I'd bet my life on it. He's fallen in love with you. I wonder if he knows it himself," Miranda said.

"Bet he doesn't." Gabby chuckled. "Although he doesn't strike me as slow. Maybe just a little *looovveee* dumbstruck."

"He does have that look about him," Roxanna added.

"Stop it!" Lily said. "I'm standing right here. You all have gone off the deep end. In love, my ass."

"Ha!" said Miranda. "That's the Lily I know. I'm so happy to see your attitude back, but I disagree with you. He's absolutely in love with you. Gabby's right — nothing about his life in Berlin, not the big deals, not the billions of dollars means anything to him compared to you. We all know he's wealthy. And yes, those jobs gave him a sense of power. But he was miserable when he arrived. Shadowed by guilt, still harboring shame for being T.D.'s son. Worried that we'd all be angry with him. He bled lonely. Since he's been back, his shadows are gone. He smiles, he's interested in the plans for this place. He's been building barns and shoveling manure, for God's sake. Most importantly he can't hide the way he looks at you."

Lily opened her mouth to speak but was too shocked. Turner had told her much of the same earlier. "People don't give all that up for a person," she said, trying to convince herself. Or shield herself.

"They do if the person's worth it. I did. I had an important job. I was in charge of my own everything. Then I met Cruz and I realized how blah and lonely my days *and nights* were without him. I gave it all up for him and I'd do it again in a heartbeat," Miranda said. "Because what I gained is worth so much more than what I had."

Lily slouched into the bar stool and put her head down on the counter, letting the cool surface calm her overheated cheek. Miranda *had* done that for Cruz. Lily had watched it happen. Her friends were in love and ready to be married. "I don't feel good," she said. "I need a drink. I need to lie down. I've never been this afraid of anything in my life. I don't do afraid. I grab adventure and passion and feast on them. This feeling, what he does to me, it makes me edgy and doubtful. Shit, I'm a complete mess."

Her friends put their arms out to her and Roxanna said, "You're not a mess, honey. You just don't know how to unlock that piece of your heart you've kept secret from him for so long. But you'll figure it out." Was Roxanna right? She'd exposed a lot to Turner today, but was she still keeping a part of her sealed? She wanted to give him everything.

"In the meantime, can we go sit on the porch, giggle and talk about the way he looks at you like he wants to steal you away to some velvet lair and make love to you forever?" Gabby asked, pinching Lily's side gently.

"I love you girls," Lily said.

"We know," Miranda said.

The four of them crammed together on the porch swing in the dark to listen and watch the men and kids at the fire pit.

"I told him about that day in high school," Lily whispered.

"You didn't!" Roxanna said.

"Wait, what day? Fill me in," Miranda ordered.

"It's so embarrassing," Lily said.

"Spill it," Gabby said. "Or we call Turner over and tell him you're smitten with him."

"Fine! Junior year, I was walking home one day when a football player started harassing me. It was getting freaky. Lord knows what he was planning. But Turner came upon us, fought him off and scared him away."

"Holy cow!" Miranda said. "Why am I only hearing of this right now?"

"Shush. I didn't know either and I've been friends with her since high school," Gabby said. "You don't usually keep secrets, Lily. Why this one? I mean, it seems like Turner saved you. Like you'd want to brag to the world."

"After, Turner walked me home and he was a jerk the entire time. He lectured, yelled, made me feel about an inch tall. With a condescending scowl on his face. I was so hurt and mortified I didn't tell anyone except Rox. Then he was gone and none of it mattered anyway."

"Is that why you get your hackles up whenever he's around?" Miranda asked.

"Partly," Lily said. "I mean, it hurt then, but I think what was more painful was that he didn't remember any of it. Didn't remember me. I kept thinking he's so damn cocky and stuck up that of course he wouldn't remember such an insignificant moment for him."

"Ahh," Miranda said. "So, you were pissed at him, and you were pissed because he didn't even know why you were pissed so you couldn't even enjoy the effect of your pissed-off-ness?"

"Damn, Miranda! You are good," Gabby said.

"What made you tell him today?" Roxanna asked.

"He spent the night last night. I left before he was awake this morning to go hide in the theater, and he found me. He was all angry and pushy," Lily said really quietly.

"Wow," Miranda whispered.

They rocked for a minute and drank their coffee, letting the outside sounds surround them. Now her friends knew about her feelings for Turner, how afraid she was. Which meant they also knew she didn't have a clue what to do with the emotions from the day.

"What did he say?" Roxanna asked.

"As I described it, the memory came back to him and he apologized and admitted that he was an egotistical, immature teenager with a chip on his shoulder who couldn't see past his anger and disgust over his father."

"Oh, I like him even more, Lily," Miranda said, squeezing Lily's hand.

"Me too." Lily held tight to the warmth of her friend.

"So," Gabby whispered after a few moments, "does he or does he not have wicked hands?"

Lily exhaled the breath she'd been holding, grateful for her friend's ability to lighten the mood. "Extremely," Lily whispered, causing the others to burst out laughing again.

* * * *

"You ladies look cozy." Turner stepped onto the dark porch. The four of them were snuggled up together. Although he couldn't make out what they'd been saying, he'd heard their giggles carrying out over the calm night air.

"Mind if I steal Lily away?" He reached his hand out to her before he realized she was asleep, her head on Roxanna's shoulder. "She's awful pretty when she's asleep and not yelling at me," he whispered, lifting her up.

The other ladies sighed when Lily was startled awake in his arms.

"Turner, what are you doing? Put me down."

"Although, then I don't get to see her eyes shoot to flame when I annoy her."

Lily rolled her eyes. Turner walked her through the house. She relaxed into him and wrapped her arms around his neck. Best fucking feeling in the world, her placing her trust in him. He'd take it, as she gave it, small moment by small moment. He'd build a foundation for her. Until she believed she could fly with her feelings for him and he'd catch her on the way down.

"I had fun tonight," she said.

He settled her into his truck. "Good. Night's not over yet."

"Turner?" she said.

"Lily."

"What's going on here?"

"I told you earlier, I'm driving you home so I can make love to you, fall asleep next to you, wake up with you in my arms, fix you breakfast and kiss you senseless before you go to work. Maybe I'll convince you to stay in bed with me all day. I'll repeat those words, if you need me to, but I'd rather show you."

"Oh." She let out a breath. "I mean you and me? The nice words, the flowers, the pastries, the long simmering looks, the way you feast on my body? Everything that's happening between us."

He knew what she meant, but he also knew that she'd probably freak out if he told her what was going on for him. That he was in love with her. That they belonged to each other, and he planned to make their arrangement permanent with a ring, marriage, family. The whole package. He didn't know when the right time would be, but he sensed it was too early for her to hear. For all her fiery nature and outspoken attitude, underneath the surface, her heart was still very fragile. He needed to tread lightly.

"I'm trying to seduce you, Lily. Is it working?" he asked. They pulled up to her house.

Neither one of them made a move to get out of the truck. Turner took her hand. "Lily?" He was prepared for another heavy moment like the one in the middle of on the lawn before dinner. And even though he was aching to get her naked so he could be inside her, he'd wait because these moments when she shared glimpses of that fragile heart with him were what made him fall in love. Patience wasn't a chore with her. It meant getting all the good stuff. He'd wait forever for her.

All thoughts of being patient flew out of the open window of his truck when she climbed over to him and fitted her body onto his lap, her back up against the steering wheel. She fused her mouth to his and kissed *him* senseless, lapping him up as though she'd been searching for years for him. They were the oasis to each other's desert.

It only took him seconds to recover. He reached around and grabbed her waist while he opened the door and lifted her out with the other hand. She wrapped her legs around him and he carried her into the house.

"Pool," she said on a breath before she kissed him again and tangled her fingers in his hair.

"Pool?" he asked, barely hanging on by a thread. He didn't give a fuck about the pool. He wanted her naked in bed, so he could love every inch of her skin.

"I've never made love in my pool before," she whispered in his ear right before she started teasing his neck with her soft, intent lips and a sneak of her tongue. All the sensations shot right to his cock.

He nearly dropped her. Thankfully her body was fused to his and she didn't seem like she'd be letting go any time soon. Stepping out onto her back deck, he set her down long enough to drag her dress up and over her head.

"Fuck, Lily. You're killing me." His heart nearly stopped. Once again, she stood naked before him under the moonlight. And the way she smiled, he knew she'd done it on purpose this time for him. This dichotomy of her, how open and free she was with her body, how she guarded her heart. Fierce and strong. Brave and sensual. One fucking heady combination.

"I like the way it feels," she teased with that soft voice of hers. "Not having much on underneath. Plus…" She stepped out of her shoes and ran her hands underneath his shirt. "I knew you'd like it. Your eyes go all dark and heavy too, like a warrior."

He tore off his clothes, picked her up and walked right down the pool steps into the water. She slid down his body, but kept her hands around his neck and her mouth on his. She'd never kissed him so powerfully before. Conversation might not be her strong suit where they were concerned, but hell, this was another way of communicating and she excelled at it, giving herself over to him.

Their bodies danced to their own music, sliding against each other, her breasts teasing his skin. He wanted to touch them, but he'd have to let go of her, and his hands were pretty damn happy where they were, kneading her ass. He traced down over the rounded edge, teasing, a caress that he'd learned made her shudder and writhe. So honest was she in her reactions, her need, her desires. She rubbed in closer. With each move, his cock surged against her body, seeking its own perfect fit. He could stay like this forever, her fingers digging into his shoulders, her mouth loving his, their bodies trying to become one.

"Turner," she breathed into his ear as she dragged a hand down to tease the indentation of his hip, dipping closer, but never reaching her target — on purpose. Damn, she nearly made him come with her words full of desire and that fucking caress that drove him wilder that if she *had* met her target. *Drugging me instead with the anticipation.* "Come inside me, bare. I'm clean and safe." She trailed her lips down his jaw, nipping and kissing.

He gripped her harder. *Christ, yes.* He'd never even allowed himself that fantasy. "I'm clean, too. You sure?"

She continued her dance against his body in wanton flaunting. *Gorgeous fucking flaunting.* Pulling herself up, she zeroed in and her aim was true as she rubbed her thumb over the tip of his cock, moaning along with him. It was as if she lost herself in giving him pleasure. With soft, strong fingers she toyed with him. He almost let her stay distracted, but he wanted inside her now.

There'd be time later for lingering. Lifting her legs up, he curled them around his waist, pushed her hand out of the way and fit himself right at her entrance, doing his own teasing while she tried to connect them. *Fuck!* It was too much and not enough. He plunged into her, lifting her hips with his hands then riding her back down onto him.

She dug her nails into his shoulders and tried, as he did, to bring them as close as possible. He fused his mouth over one of her nipples, sucking on it, hard. Her moans were so sweet and sexy to his ears. God, when she let herself feel and shared that with him, when she let herself come apart in his arms, completely vulnerable and passionate, he'd swear he'd never seen anything more beautiful.

He lost himself in her too, diving over the edge. He buried his face in her neck and chest, kissing and tasting her. The world went hazy around him.

Unsure how he managed to stay standing, he swayed with her in the water, loving the way she was wrapped around him. The underwater pool lights played around her body with the moonlight, flickering and shining their own seductive dance. When he finally slid out of her, she moaned again, this time with a pout on her lips. He'd seen her angry, pissed, apologetic, sad, happy, but the pout made him grin. Her mouth was all emotion, like her eyes. Hell, like her entire being. No wonder she'd become an artist who worked with her hands and her body to build beautiful things. That kind of talent and passion were more powerful than words any day for someone like Lily. She gave power to her emotions through her art. It was another thing he loved about her.

Turner rested her back against his chest and let her float. "Sorry I was so fast, Liliana."

"Mmm," she murmured, and he could hear the smile evident in her voice. "That was amazing, Turner. I like that you can't control yourself around me." She turned her head into his neck and kissed him right before she nipped at his earlobe with her teeth.

"Tease." He pinched her side.

She laughed and swam from his arms, climbed on his back and attempted to dunk him. But he easily had her under the water before she could blink. When she surfaced, sputtering and laughing, he dragged her body tight to his.

"Don't let me go," she said, the tease in her expression gone. He huffed at the serious pleading in her eyes. *Giving me one more small part of herself, trusting me.*

"Never." *I'm never letting you go.* He carried her out of the pool and into her shower where with careful hands he soaped her body and, lingering over each precious inch, washed her. The beauty was that she simply let go and let Turner cherish her.

Chapter Twenty-Three

Lily woke with the sun, slowly, gradually stretching limbs, from darkness to bold hints of color. Even with her eyes still closed, she could guess the time of day, close to six. The birds were gossiping before the rest of the world intruded on their quiet air. One lone float plane soared overhead. Distant waves played in the wind. Sunlight flickered through her gauzy curtains and over the thin cells of her eyelids and...coffee. Mmm, she smelled coffee. Sweet heaven it was close. Closer than her coffeemaker all the way in her kitchen. She imagined her first cup, with the right amount of heavy cream, and took in a deep breath of contentment. Oh, that aroma of coffee was almost, *almost* better than Turner's scent mixed with the scent of her sheets, which brought a giddy smile to her face.

He'd done what he'd promised—he'd brought her home, made love to her, slept with her. Actually—she put her hand on her fluttering heart—he'd done so much more than words could describe, and...wait, where was he? Her eyes shot open when Turner fitted his warm, naked body against hers from behind.

"Morning." Turner's rough, low voice thrilled in her ear. His arm reached over her to set a huge mug of coffee on her side table. She followed the mug with her sleepy, happy eyes, but was forced to look away from her mug of deliciousness.

"Coffee," she called toward it when Turner rolled her to her back then snuggled on top of her. Yes, the hot prodigal son snuggled. Mmm, snuggling was so good. She wrapped her hands around him when he kissed her. Even his kiss was soft, kneading in for comfort and he tasted like coffee. The sneak had already had some. *Sexy sneak*. Sexy turned to scorching. He slowly tasted her and moved his body over hers. A hard, warm body over her sleepy, sated one. And suddenly she wasn't so sleepy anymore. Turner Brockman was way better than coffee.

* * * *

Later, when the sun was high and she had no idea what time it was anymore—nor did she care—she sat in her kitchen nook in a soft robe and watched him cook. Turner made another fresh pot of coffee and delivered a mug to her, loaded with cream. Jeans and bare feet again, but this time he was shirtless. Much better, but she wondered why they'd ever gotten out of bed. Although, taking a sip, she decided it was the best cup of delayed coffee she'd ever had. Made even better since she got to ogle him in her kitchen. He did belong there. He belonged in her world. He may have snuck in under her radar, or maybe he felt like he'd been beating down her walls with a pickax, but he was there and she wanted him to stay.

He made her some sort of fluffy pancake full of berries artfully topped with a light dusting of powdered sugar. The smell was incredible, warm jam meeting caramelized doughy, cakey goodness. Immediately she took the powdered sugar shaker he'd set on the table and added the *correct* amount of sugar. She caught his grin at her antics and didn't feel one bit embarrassed.

"You missed a spot," he teased. The entire thing was now sugar-white on top.

"Wait till you taste it. Sugar makes everything better." She pouted and was rewarded when he slid in next to her and melted her pout away with his closeness. She didn't know whether to taste *him* or the pancake. She had ignored coffee for him earlier and it had been so, *so* worth it. Hmm, and he smelled good. He'd showered after they'd gotten up the second time, but what he smelled like now was sugar and hot butter in a pan. In a word, delicious. She leaned in and kissed him.

Yes, oh, yes, good choice. She mentally patted herself on the back when he more than leaned in too, hungry for her. He put his hand behind her head so she wouldn't fall and when she opened for him, his tongue teased her lips, driving her crazy. Then even though she could feel his banked desire through his hand and his chest, he savored her slowly. She reached out to grab onto his shirt to pull him closer. Only she couldn't find purchase because the man was nearly naked. Well, then she'd just have to climb on. That had worked last night. She started to when he stopped kissing her and pulled his lips away. She whimpered. *And is he chuckling?*

"Did you just laugh at me, Turner Brockman?" she asked, practically draped over him while he held her hands. *God, am I panting? Or drooling? Maybe both?*

"You need food, gorgeous," he said, placing one more soft kiss on her lips with his eyes wide open. Mmm, he had such pretty eyes. She could get lost in those jade depths.

"What?" She blinked and for one tiny second, she could see all the way inside him to his soul. Passionate, desiring, intent, at peace and hers. Her soulmate. Having no idea he'd just shattered all her reservations, he arranged her so her back was to his front. And he fed her.

Oh, she thought, her emotions and head were upside down. She swallowed back her joyful tears. Right, this delicious *pan kuchen* or whatever he'd called it. "Ohmygdturnr." She closed her eyes and moaned then gobbled up another bite. She was almost sad to share, except when his gorgeous lips took a taste, the shiver it sent through her was far better that having it all to herself "Why have I never had this before? And all that extra sugar I added, warm sugary lusciousness."

"Good, huh?"

"Uh, good?" He ate mechanically, except for his eyes which were focused on her, as if she was the sun and he served her, even if her rays would burn him to the ground. Like he wanted her to burn him to the ground. He'd gone from relaxed and laughing to tense. "It's the best damn thing I've ever tasted. I could eat this every morning, Turner."

She quickly opened for the next bite he held for her. Another whimper of delight escaped her body. Dough, sugar, berries — the taste had her entire body moving in tempo. His head was so close to hers she could feel his breath on her neck. He reached to fork another bite for her and at the same time placed his lips on her neck. Whew! He was making her dizzy. Especially when he licked down the column in one tortuous taste and nuzzled the robe off her shoulder with his head so he could kiss her bare skin. One hand fed her while the other snuck around, untied her robe and worked inside to her breasts. Biting down on the sugary sweet goodness, Lily closed her eyes and moaned, from his touch, from the taste, the most amazing combination.

"Fuck! Those moans of yours drive me crazy." *Annndd* she was done eating. Turner made a painful sound that sounded like a growl, dropped the fork and tugged her robe all the way off. He wasn't tense anymore. No, he unleashed his desire upon her.

Then, *then* he let her on his lap. Okay, not so much *let* as dragged her over him, her knees bent on either side of him. He palmed her breasts with his gorgeous, large hands, and scattered kisses all over her naked chest. His skin always felt hot to her cold, such an intense combination. Greedy for him, too, she ran her fingers down his back, molding her body to his. She buried her head in his neck, sniffed his sexy sugar man scent then trailed her tongue over the soft skin. When she used her teeth, he surged up with her in his arms and stumbled to the sofa.

"Need to be inside you." He tugged off his jeans. "Tried to be patient and feed you. Never knew how sexy watching you eat could be. You could kill a man from desire." But he didn't come inside her, not right away. He sent his masterful hands all over her body. Every rough patch on his fingers, every callous sparking over her skin. A match lit here, and there. Another spark set free, until he moved her knees apart and after one hot sear from his eyes, he put his mouth on her core and tasted her.

"God, Turner!" Then she lost her words. If he hadn't been holding her, she would have bucked off the couch. This was…no one had ever…not like this… He sucked and teased, alternating from gentle kisses to darting his wicked tongue on her. His mouth was extraordinary coupled with his thumbs rubbing the delicate skin of her inner thighs. It was incredible and vulnerable at the same time to be so spread open, so worshiped. Every inch of her he touched went up in flame. The grip he had on her hips, his erotic thumbs, the movement of his entire body savoring hers... She let herself feel everything the way the flames surged together. Higher until she was shaking, nearly crying with need.

Finally, he shattered her, feasting at the same time he destroyed her. As she came down, he soothed her with soft kisses, even softer promises. His words and lips sent a murmur through her. Then he climbed on top of her, a hot, growly animal, needy, like her. She met his body with her own. Wrapping her legs around him, she blushed under his attention. He placed himself at her entrance and surged inside. There were no gentle pauses. He clasped her hands in his, rubbed her own calloused fingers with his larger ones, making every inch of her body feel beautiful. He fused his lips to hers and the rest of his body met her power. They urged each other closer until she exploded again all around him, bucking in a frenzy when her climax burst through her.

"Fucking beautiful." He kept up his pace, thrusting inside her until it was too much even for him to prolong and she got to watch his entire body tighten and shudder with his release, his muscles rolling like waves in a storm.

He's the beautiful one. Exactly like this, *powerful, free, loving.* Lily felt their racing hearts calm, with him collapsed mostly on top of her. *Loving.* It didn't scare her so much when she tried to word out in her mind. In fact, it made her feel a million feet tall and lighter than air, giddy. She wanted to scream from the rooftops how amazing it felt. Turner rolled them slightly so they were facing each other, but he didn't let go. If anything, he wrapped his arms tighter around her. Through his heavy breaths, she felt him smile against her neck and rumble, "Never moving from this spot. And…" He placed a soft kiss right on her lips.

"And?" she asked, wondering what was going to come out of his mouth next.

"And, I know what I'm getting you for Christmas. More of those powdered sugar shakers."

Lily laughed and let out a breath of nerves, letting them go for good. She squeezed him back, wondering if there was any way they could get even closer. Independence was one thing, and she'd certainly mastered it, proven to the world that she excelled at it. *But connection is everything*, she thought. His lips, his body, his sense of humor, his love. *He is my everything*.

He played with her ridiculous curls, curls she had no control over, and asked, "What's on your agenda for the day?"

"Hmm." She pulled back to take him in. "More of this, pretty please." And she watched a satisfied smile spread over his face. He'd earned it. "Although…" She yawned. "Can we nap in between?" A lazy Sunday sounded perfect to her. "Oh!" She sat up abruptly, using Turner's hip to rest her hand on. His naked hip that led to…

Shit! She tried to untangle her thoughts and her body. Instead she fell off the couch onto her soft rug. At least she got to listen to Turner's laugh. The man had a sexy deep laugh, as if he hadn't laughed in a long, long time, storing them up for something special. And now he gave them to her daily as gifts. She was going to start demanding them, because she knew she would never get enough. And how precious to know he laughed with her because he was unafraid to be himself. All those years living with a demon for a father. Some might call it a miracle how he'd turned out to be such a good man. She knew it was his strength, his will, his heart. How blessed she'd been to have parents who adored her.

"I need to visit my papá today."

Turner quit laughing, helped her up and wrapped his body around her again. She loved how affectionate he was. Like he couldn't get enough of her. "Want some company?"

Lily only had to consider his question for a moment before she nodded and let Turner hug her. Her father slept so much these days that he most likely wouldn't even know Turner was there. But Lily would. And selfish of her or not, she was the one who needed Turner now, needed the support. She could barely swallow with the knowledge that she wouldn't have to face the shittiest part of her days — watching her father deteriorate before her eyes — alone.

Chapter Twenty-Four

On one hand, Turner was relieved to finally have a meeting with Ms. Wells from Premier. On the other, his weird gut feeling along with the fact that she was thirty minutes late had put a spoiler on his spectacular high. A high from being in love. He'd loved Lily even when she'd been guarded and pushed him away or, rather, run from him. Now, watching her struggle through her fears, admit why she was mad at him from the beginning in all her glorious vulnerability then bare herself completely to him had been spectacular. Finally, she'd placed her trust in him. She'd let him in to a past where he'd unintentionally hurt her. Accepted his apology. And she'd chased away so many of his past ghosts. He hadn't realized how much he needed her to believe in him, to believe that he was nothing like T.D. Brockman. It made it easier to believe himself when he had a fierce goddess on his side.

Love was fucking phenomenal. Jesus, he couldn't wait to begin their life together. He felt like someone with a terminal disease who'd been cured. A second chance on life. He hadn't been living before, not fully. Now, he was never wasting another moment.

Going with her to see her dad. He hadn't said much because he'd had to choke back his emotion. Fuck, Mr. Moreno was unrecognizable. Once towering over all of them in height and size, he'd had the strength of a giant and the disposition of a gentle man full of kindness and laughter. Now his home was a hospital bed, his body withered and gray. He hadn't opened his eyes once while they were there. Turner wondered which was worse for Lily, when her father remained asleep the entire visit or when he was awake but lost to her.

How the fuck had Lily kept her shit together through all this?

She could teach him so much about being brave and facing down her fears, all the while keeping her chin up and her attitude at level ten. He was even more determined to understand the issue of her father's hardware store. Based on what the nurse he spoke to said, no way in hell would her father have been making sound decisions at the time he'd supposedly signed the deed over to T.D. Brockman. Thank God that devil was in the ground where he belonged. Thank God he couldn't hurt anyone anymore.

Now, Turner just needed to solve the ownership mystery, take control over what belonged to him and his brothers and Lily, and focus on living a fabulous life with her in Graciella, their home together. They'd had two glorious weeks since she'd put down all her walls. He'd spent every night at her place. Once or twice he'd successfully kissed her back to bed after their morning shower, before they were forced to separate for the day so they could both get to work.

Today, this meeting was first on his agenda and he did not like being kept waiting.

"Ahh." A long sigh—like a cat who'd discovered a nest full of baby birds and devoured said birds—came from a harsh-looking woman strolling down the sidewalk toward him. "You must be Turner Brockman, prodigal son returned home after ruling the international world of finance and development."

It was a battle not to roll his eyes, but Turner managed. He could keep a game face. He held out his hand in a gesture of politeness, but would have rather abstained. She wasn't the first realtor who'd given him a disgusting feeling.

"Ms. Wells." Turner crossed his arms when she moved in closer. "Been waiting for this meeting. Mind if we get started?" *Get it over with, more like.* He could put her in her place, watch her skedaddle out of town then hand Lily the deed to her father's store as the rightful owner.

"Absolutely," she purred. "When I heard your name on my messages, I cleared my schedule and raced back to Graciella." She unlocked the door to her building and stepped inside. "To be honest, I was working a deal in Los Angeles for the properties, but I'm sure you know how persuasive the name Klein Development is. Shall we talk numbers?"

"Excuse me?" Turner was here for one reason only—to untangle the mess T.D. had left him. Separating the land and the buildings had been a shitshow for Cruz and Jake to figure out, not to mention Miranda, when she'd conducted the audit. And he couldn't imagine how Adam had felt, being left out of the will completely. The one brother who truly deserved to inherit everything. Now Turner could finally help his brothers, help Lily, help the entire town move on from T.D.'s ugly shadow.

"I know it seems unlikely in a teeny Podunk town like this, but you are in for a surprise."

I'm not the only one, he thought smugly.

"What I have for you is going to blow your mind from a development standpoint. Several properties on this side of the street are for sale. There are a few in between I'm sure you could get your hands on with the right incentive. And I think it's perfect for one of your projects, knocking everything down and building big, glossy and expensive. A massive hotel and convention center. Mall on one end. Mixed use with restaurants, bars...the hotel could be high enough that the pampered guests could get a view of the Pacific. Add a spa, maybe clear the streets behind eventually and add a golf course. I can see it all now. Money, money, money."

A monstrosity of a high-rise? A *mall* in the middle of downtown Graciella? *Hell no.* "T.D. left these buildings to me. I don't know who you are or how you think you're involved, but the only reason I'm here is to get the deeds I assume you have and end your time in Graciella permanently."

Her purr turned to near hissing. "I'm T.D.'s partner."

"Well, now that T.D.'s dead, he doesn't have any partners." Turner spoke slowly to control his temper. "I'm sure you figured that out. I'd like all the deeds. Then we can be finished."

"Oh, Turner." She laughed and the purr was back, but different. It certainly wasn't the sound of someone about to lose millions of dollars in development in a seaside town. "Your father sold the Graciella properties to me. Signed each and every contract right before he died. I would have purchased your precious family farm too if I could have afforded it. So, legally, I guess you're correct. T.D. doesn't have any partners. But you're also wrong. He didn't leave these to you, because I own them all. No more partners at all. Doesn't feel good to be wrong, does it?" The words slithered out of her.

What the fuck?

And, placing all the contracts on the table, she continued to shred his world. He studied them, and from what he could tell, they were legitimate. His father's signature was there. They were dated days before his death, and each one had been notarized. Fuck, had someone slammed him onto the cement? He wanted to punch the wall. He wanted T.D. to be alive so he could pummel him into the ground for all the pain he'd caused everyone. Turner hadn't been this angry and powerless since he was a teenager. The writing on the contracts swam before his eyes and he calmed his temper. Talked himself down from the edge of rage. At least he wasn't still an impulsive eighteen-year-old. Thinking he could run, push the past behind in and forget it all forever. "Explain, now."

"No." Her frosty voice cut through his mental battle. "I'm going to sell to the highest bidder. *Then*, I will leave this little town and never return." She placed the contracts back in her briefcase and snapped it shut with a smug look on her face. "Feel free to keep that one. I'm sure you're going to read through ever teeny, tiny legal word. I had a copy made especially for you."

She made her way to the door and gave him her ruthless smile one last time. "If you change your mind about buying them, you know how to get hold of me.

But remember, Turner Brockman, a sale can be pulled right out from under your feet faster than you can blink. I suggest not wasting one second figuring out your strategy. Don't bother locking up. I won't be back to this stupid office."

Turner stood in the silent, empty building, anger rolling off him, wondering how in the hell he was going to fix this problem.

Chapter Twenty-Five

For the first time in a long time, Lily wasn't racing somewhere. She was floating. The theater was nearly done. *Hard to believe.* She'd been so deep in the journey of perfecting it and, although she'd pictured people filling the seats and enjoying movies, she hadn't really imagined the small quiet in between when she completed the makeover to when it would burst to life with an audience. One grand polish was all it needed now. And she would do it herself, clean and shine every last corner of her baby. She'd already planned an opening party in her mind. All she had to do was figure out which movie would be the inaugural one. It had to be something special, with love and a happy ending, a bit of flair. Maybe an old Audrey Hepburn, or Sophia Loren. Maybe a dash of intrigue and suspense.

She was proud of herself. Now arriving at Brockman House to see the windows installed and siding up nearly made her cry with pride in her employees. Her crew was phenomenal. It would be completed by September, possibly before, if they kept up their pace.

She'd gone home and cleaned up before meeting Turner here. Sexy jeans and a frilly blouse to shake things up a bit. She added a few sparkly bobby pins to her hair because she felt sparkly. Also, easier access for him to kiss her ears that way he did so softly like a feather. Who knew ears could be so erogenous? He was taking her out. Well, technically they weren't going out at all. He was cooking for her and they were eating on the lawn under the lights. But this time only the two of them. Maybe she'd get lucky in Turner's bed later. Another silly girlhood dream come true. Her face flushed with what they could get up to in his bed. She was early, couldn't hide her excitement at being near him again.

Free of burdens was a fabulous place to be. It made her want to skip. Suddenly she didn't have to scowl and wonder what game he might be playing, battle between wanting him and not wanting to want him. Or hide her secret wounds from him. All she needed was a mountain and she could twirl like Maria in *The Sound of Music*. Instead of, "The hills are alive," she'd sing, "He wants to stay." Good thing her livelihood wasn't based on her song lyrics. She giggled at the thought. But the words made her happy.

He'd opened his soul to her when he'd spoken of his complicated feelings toward T.D. and he'd opened his heart when vowing he wanted to stay with her in Graciella. After all he'd been through, all the baggage he'd carried around alone since childhood, he'd still turned into a beautiful, loving man who gave his trust over to her easily. Or maybe not easily. Maybe he knew she was the one. And he was her one. She could give him all her thoughts, her worries, her dreams and especially her heart and he would cherish every precious piece.

How amazing to be in love, openly. She was in love with Turner Brockman and she was pretty sure he loved her back. *That's what dreams are made of.*

She walked around to the back porch to put her bag down and tuck the bottle of white she'd brought into the kitchen fridge before she went to find Turner with his brothers down at the barn.

She liked surprising him, and she really liked finding him all dirty and sweaty, her sexy rancher. He could get her all messy. Then they could clean each other together. Mmm, shower sex with Turner Brockman. It was becoming one of her favorites. *Nope, this girl doesn't have to dream anymore. The man is all mine.*

"I have to go. Those properties for sale… This is the deal of a lifetime. For me, for all of us. I feel like my entire career has been practice for this and nothing else matters. I can't *not* be there. It affects the entire west side of Main Street." *Turner's not at the barns.* His impassioned words came to her from the kitchen as she stepped onto the back porch. And all her blood rushed to her head. *Main Street, my Main Street? For sale? Papá's store?*

"I get it," Cruz said, "I'd want to be present for the sale too. Although it's probably good I'm not going. You'd have to hold me back from tackling that woman. Just, please explain to Lily before you go."

Explain? Where is he going? He told her he would figure out what was happening with her father's hardware store and get it back to her. He promised. *Sale? Huge deal?* A lit fuse buzzed in her head. *Which properties on that side of the street is he talking about?* Lily sucked in a breath. *It can't be the hardware.*

"I'm with Cruz on that." Adam laughed. His voice teasing, playful. "You can't just run away on her again."

He said he wanted to stay. An ice pick carved into her heart. A boot smashed into her gut. She leaned against the doorjamb to keep from falling. *Nothing else matters?*

"I'm not running away, idiot. I'll tell her where I'm going. I just don't want to tell her *why* until everything is solved. She has enough to worry about."

"Seriously though, this is a huge development. Don't keep this from her."

"Look, I trust Hans—he wouldn't tell me he has the sale in the bag if he didn't. But I want to wait until the deal is done, all paperwork signed before I tell Lily anything. I want proof."

Hans Klein, Turner's boss, who destroys old structures and puts up ugly, cold monstrosities. Not in my town. Oh, hell no! "What the hell?" Lily braced herself in the doorway. Sucked in breaths, but it felt like fire in her lungs.

"Lily." Turner started toward her with a smile. *A smile?* Boom! The dynamite in her head exploded.

She barreled into his space and shoved him. "Wipe that damned smile off your face, Turner Brockman. You are unfucking believable!"

"Lily, wait." He grabbed her arms to hold her back, but in her rage she was stronger. She pulled away and smacked his chest when he grabbed her around the waist this time, pinning her arms between them. "Let me explain."

"You lied to me! Told me you were staying, that you would get my father's store back. To me. It belongs to me." She kicked at his shins with her heels until he dropped her. "You *betrayed* me. My father's hardware store means nothing to you. This entire town means nothing to you. I mean nothing to you."

"None of that is true. Calm down and let me—"

"Calm down? I won't *calm* down. Don't fucking patronize me!" She backed away. Her heart tried to smash out of her chest.

Turner shook his head, took a step closer. "I didn't mean it like that. I can explain."

"I don't need your shitty explanations. I get it. You saw one more money-making development and had to get in on it. Does it mean *nothing* to you that it's Graciella? My home, your *home*? Oh, God, you're not home. Are you? Shit! I've been so stupid. You never planned on staying. And us?" Words flew out of her like wasps from a nest on fire. "You didn't have to lie to get me into bed. I would have been perfectly fine with a meaningless affair. At least we would have been on even playing field."

Turner flinched.

"Oh, no, you do not get to act hurt! You seduced me. Worse, you pretended to care for me, made me feel precious, made me *trust* you."

"Lily," he pleaded. "Nothing was pretend."

"It's not what you think, Lily." Cruz tried to interrupt. Calm, obnoxious fucking older brother. And she was done.

"You two." She whirled on Adam and Cruz who looked at her like she was a crazy person. She was crazy. What the hell had she been thinking? That this was her family? She had no family. Not anymore. "You should be ashamed of yourselves. Selling off those properties, now that you have all you need right here on your perfect farm. Well, let me tell you, that town means everything to some of us, and you all...what?

215

Sold us out?" Her voice was gone, hoarse and empty. Anger coursed through her. She was shaking. She'd never been consumed by rage and stabbing pain at the same time before. How in the hell could she have been swindled by all three of them?

"Lily, you know us. You know that's not true—" Adam started.

"You *are* like your father," she hissed. "All three of you. Exactly like him. No, worse because you made me feel beloved, a part of your family. T.D. never went that far. I hope you all rot in hell!"

Get out. She had to get the hell out. And she turned and ran stumbling while Turner chased her. Frantic and fast she reached her truck first and tore away from the farm, maybe for the last time ever.

It wasn't until she was home that she broke. The drive was a blur. Climbing out of the truck, she crumbled, her face covered in tears. She scrambled up, shut herself in her bedroom, buried under the covers and wrapped herself in a ball, trying like hell to catch her heart before every part bled out of her body.

What in the actual fuck just happened? Ignoring speed limits, Turner raced after Lily. Earlier, after his encounter with Ms. Wells, he'd gone searching for her. Lily was the first person he thought of and the first person he wanted to share everything with. But when he couldn't locate her and had time to calm, he'd decided it might be better to come up with solutions first. So he could present them to her after he told her what a pile of manure everything had turned into. No way in hell was he going to lose her father's hardware store for her. To tell her what he'd discovered would break her. She was the first person he'd made promises to and he intended to keep every single one. Instead of tracking her down to only give her shitty news, he'd dug in and started working on a plan.

Great plan! You fucked up by not finding her immediately after learning T.D. sold her father's store to Ms. Wells. No, he would not give in to the doubts that raced through him now, that he might have ruined everything. He could salvage this. He didn't have a choice.

Her truck was home and parked, but the driver's door was ajar, and Lily nowhere in sight. She'd forgotten her truck but locked the front door to her house. *Fuck!* "Lily! Open the door, please!!" Turner yelled and pounded. She wouldn't listen to him back at the farm. He had to get her to listen. Jesus Christ, she thought *they'd* sold the buildings. How could she think they'd do that? *'You are like your father…no, worse.'* He wasn't sure which blow hurt more, those words she'd flung at all of them or when she'd insinuated everything between him and her, their love, their relationship, had been a lie. That all he'd wanted was an empty affair. That she would have been *fine* with an affair.

How could she believe any of that? How could he have let her? *Empty?* He was empty without her. How the fuck had everything gone so epically wrong in the span of an afternoon, an instant? One minute, he was discussing his plan with his brothers. The next she was attacking him, breaking his heart in the process with her words, her perception. Worse, she left hers splattered all over the kitchen floor. He'd never seen her look so completely devastated. And she thought him the cause. If he couldn't fix this, they'd both be destroyed.

"Lily," he yelled to no response. "We didn't sell the properties. *I* didn't sell them. Please let me in so I can explain. You're killing me!" Turner kept pounding, but there was nothing. No noise, no Lily screaming at him. The only thing that met his pleas was silence. God damned fucking silence. He made his way around the perimeter of her house trying all the windows and doors. Dammit he had to get her to listen. But there was a private jet waiting for him to leave out of Portland in four hours.

If he left Lily without explaining everything to her, she might never speak to him again. But if he stayed in Graciella, if he missed his flight, if he wasn't in Berlin to seal the deal, he would never be worthy of her love and trust, because he might not be able to get her father's store back. Then his betrayal would be real, not a shitty misunderstanding.

Turner called Cruz, his hand shaking with fear. He hadn't felt this powerless since he was a child. A stupid kid with a chip on his shoulder. A stupid kid who wanted love from a shitty father. Now, here was this beautiful, sensitive woman had opened his heart to healthy love and he might lose her completely.

"She won't let me in," he bit out. "I know, but I can't leave her like this." Yelling was getting him nowhere. "Right. Please. I owe you one. And, Cruz...love you, man."

Turner hung up and pounded one last time on Lily's door. This time his words were whispered as if he could will his love into her. "Please don't give up on us. This is the most beautiful life, one with you in it, one with you loving me. I love you so much. And I'll be back for you, Liliana Moreno. I promise."

Chapter Twenty-Six

It's hours later, Lily thought. She wasn't exactly sure what time it was in her fuzzy brain. She woke to a room full of afternoon light. Blinding, unforgiving light. Jesus, when had she ever thought waking to the sunlight was a good thing? Her entire body ached from sleeping in the same tense position she'd curled herself into when she'd made it home, or maybe from her heart shattering into a million pieces.

No, no, no, no. She refused to be broken-hearted. Liliana Moreno might get knocked down in life, but she certainly didn't let some soulless man break her heart. Especially not twice in one lifetime. She'd just rest a little more. Later she'd get up and clean the hell out of her theater, make it shine the way she intended. She turned on her back, attempted to stretch and...

"What in the hell!" she screamed and flung herself off the bed, landing on her beautiful, hardwood floors. *Ouch!* It was official, they were hard wood all right. The woven wool rug did nothing to cushion the blow to her beaten-up body. She crawled back onto the bed next to

Roxanna, who was propped up, nursing her *bambina*. "What are you doing here?" she asked softer this time. Serafina pulled away from Roxanna's breast, all sound asleep, milk-drunk, open-mouthed, precious baby girl.

"Uh." Roxanna stared at her. "We heard about what happened, then you went missing, honey. We came to check on you, take care of you. It's not every day my best friend thinks she gets her heart broken and completely falls apart."

"Oh." Lily waved her hand. "I'm perfectly fine." She had to choke out the last word. But she would be fine. Soon. In a few minutes. Maybe after one more nap. No broken anything for her. She would deny it forever. *Because that's how long it'll take to get over this feeling.* "Fine, fine, fine." Although, when she spoke her mouth felt full of sawdust. Sweaty curls stuck to the side of her face and her arms felt cramped and exhausted, as if she'd been physically holding herself together for hours. None of that compared to the churning in her stomach like she'd had a case of wine to herself last night. *Wine?* She'd taken wine to Turner's, but she hadn't had any to drink.

"She's awake," Miranda said, walking into the bedroom with a tray of coffee.

"Mmm hmm." Roxanna eyed Lily carefully.

Miranda handed her a mug. Lily brought it to her mouth and inhaled the nectar of the goddesses. And… *Uh-oh.* Lily took one breath, threw herself off the bed and made it to the toilet just in time, emptying her stomach into the basin. "What hell is this…what is wrong with me?" Her words were barely a whisper. And she found, when she tried, she couldn't stand up. Everything wobbled — her legs, her head, her insides.

"My expert guess? You're either pregnant or heartbroken, maybe both," Roxanna said, matter-of-fact.

"What?" Lily hissed out. "No way. Hello! On the pill here! I am definitely not pregnant, and there is no way in hell I'm broken whatever... You can't be broken heat...heart...over someone you hate with every fiber of your being." *Gosh, it's exhausting to talk. Maybe I'll slide right down on this tile floor and take a nap.*

"Let's get you back to bed." Miranda helped her stand.

"I'm tired. I was mad and I didn't get much sleep last night."

Roxanna choked on her water and, after she'd cleared her throat, said, "You've been asleep for two days, honey, almost three. That's why I used my key. Miranda and I have been taking turns staying with you. I was just getting ready to go home again."

Lily felt all the heat drain from her cheeks. "What?" She crawled back onto the bed and rested her head on her pillow. She rubbed her chest and looked at Miranda when she offered her a tissue. "That's not going to help the pain in my chest."

"You're crying," Miranda said.

Lily put a hand to her cheek and felt the wetness again. Then she looked at her friends and said, "I don't feel so good."

* * * *

After a shower and some tea Roxanna said, "Can you tell us what happened? Maybe we can help. We only heard Cruz and Adam's side. It sounded like a tsunami hit."

"I was there to have a date," she started, her throat raw. *My first date with Turner, ruined.*

"And," Miranda prodded.

"I heard them talking. They're selling T.D.'s buildings on the side of the street where the hardware store is. Some fucking deal of a lifetime for Turner. How could he? And Cruz and Adam too. All three of them. I'm so confused. I lost it. I lambasted them. I think I kind of went overboard." She looked between Miranda and Roxana, who were both stupidly quiet.

"Well, *kind of* isn't exactly how Adam put it," Roxanna said.

"Traitor," Lily grumbled, and looked down into her mug. "What was I supposed to do? They're selling Graciella buildings to some jackass in Germany. To make money. To make it some ugly splashy, institutional icky thing. It'll ruin us. How can you even be calm right now?"

"They aren't selling the buildings, Lily," Miranda said. But when Lily looked at her with hope filling her chest, Miranda's face was in turmoil.

"What? What is it?"

Miranda sat next to her. "It turns out, T.D. already sold them to a partner he had, a Ms. Wells. Right before he died. Legally they belong to her. Three of them, including the hardware store."

"No." Lily's breath drained out of her. "We're too late? Can't they fight it? I know my father was not sane enough to sell that store. There's got to be a way." Being in limbo about the hardware store had sucked, but she'd had faith that once T.D.'s estate was completely settled, everything would turn out fine. Hearing the words '*T.D. already sold them*' broke her. No wonder they could never get any answers.

"They were going to try to fight it, but Jake said based on the contract Ms. Wells left in Turner's possession, the Brockmans probably wouldn't win."

"So, what? They're just...going to turn it into the deal of a lifetime," she whispered. "Turner's company in Berlin? How easy for him to make a deal out of it. And once he's there, he'll probably realize there's nothing for him here. That's what hurts more. I fell in love with him all over again, *felt* his love, or imagined it, which is worse. Turns out it was all meaningless for him."

"Stop thinking like that, Lily." Roxanna gently smacked her hand. "Turner is one hundred percent gone, over the moon, would do anything for you. He chased you down when you left the other night, but he couldn't get you to open the door. Stood here pounding and yelling for a good half hour before he had to get to Portland for his flight to Germany."

"He did? I had no idea. I didn't even hear him. I was so, so..."

"Traumatized, it sounds like, if you really misinterpreted everything that way," Miranda said.

"Have a little faith that he will figure it out, that he'll come back to you, honey," Roxanna said.

"What if it really is the deal of a lifetime? Isn't that what he's been running toward his entire career. I don't know which will hurt worse, if he comes back to develop Graciella into a generic behemoth or if he doesn't come back at all."

"You're putting your walls back up. I think you have it all wrong," Miranda said. "He didn't just fall in love with you, my beautiful friend — he fell back in love with this town too. And he's not willing to give either one up."

Lily buried her head under her pillow and groaned. "He might be, after everything I said. What have I done? I was nasty to all three of them. What if my actions keep him away from me? What if I'm the one that ruins us?"

Chapter Twenty-Seven

Three days. He hadn't seen or spoken to Lily in three days, since she'd stormed away from him and barricaded herself alone in her fortress. It felt like three decades. Each second stretched out before him like being tortured in slow motion. She hadn't answered her phone, or her door, and hadn't returned any of his calls. Leaving without talking to her felt like drowning. Hopefully she would give him a chance when he returned. Cruz and Miranda had assured him he should go to Germany. That it was the right thing to do and that once the deal was finalized, he would be able to explain everything to her. God, he hoped they were correct. She was *everything* to him and he needed to prove that to her.

This is your chance, he told himself, walking into the small conference room where Hans was pretend-wooing Ms. Wells with hints at billions of dollars.

"Mr. Klein, it's so good to be here. I'd love to see your offer. You made it sound impossible to turn down on the phone and with the first-class flight and fabulous hotel. It must be something special."

"Of course, Ms. Wells. Here's my colleague with it now." Hans stood. Turner walked down the length of the table and dropped a folder in front of her.

She blinked, quickly covered her surprise and smiled that same evil witchy look, confident she'd beaten them once more "Why, Mr. Brockman. How nice to see you again. Decided to get in on the deal, I see. Taking after your father. Smart boy." She patted his arm before he could pull it away. He walked to the other side of the conference table. It wasn't far enough, but it would have to do.

"Oh, I'm definitely in on the deal." Standing stoic, he refused to give her an ounce of emotion.

She read the paperwork in front of her and he took pleasure watching her face morph into anger, then disgust. Neither one looked good on her.

"You're joking." She snapped the folder closed.

"No joke," Hans said. "This is the final offer from Klein Development. Take it or leave it."

"What?" she snapped and gathered her purse. She started to walk out. "Why fly me over here only to insult me?"

"That's not the only reason we flew you here, Ms. Wells," Turner said softly. "A conversation needed to be had and now you're on my turf. Walk out that door and not only do you lose out on any deal you'll get on those properties from *anyone*, but you may lose your license and face jail time."

She stopped. "For what, selling my own properties? You've both lost your minds."

"At least two of those buildings were purchased illegally. One owner was coerced while not in his right mind and I have signed affidavits from medical doctors regarding that. In fact, we think T.D. forged several signatures where he wanted."

And her smile was back. "You can't prove any of that. Even if you could, T.D. is dead. It has nothing to do with me or the sale now."

"Oh, really. Were you or were you not T.D.'s *partner*?"

"Yes. And he sold them to me."

"We found your other partner too. The title clerk you bribed to keep the deeds from being filed. To keep us guessing and confused. Lots of laws broken by you."

"I…only…" Finally, she stumbled. *Gotcha*, Turner wanted to say, with a fist in the air.

"We're prepared financially, time wise, and with the best legal team in the world to hold any sale of those buildings up in court for an extremely long time, Ms. Wells," Hans said, pouring himself some coffee. "By all means, if you're prepared for the same, walk out that door and our lawyers will do the talking. Otherwise, this is the deal. Take it, enjoy the day in Berlin and never set foot in Graciella again."

"This is illegal, you can't — "

"No, Ms. Wells, what's illegal is forging a signature of a man so riddled with Alzheimer's he doesn't know his own name anymore. What's illegal and unethical is coercing a family to sell their corner restaurant in order to pay for their child's medical bills. What's illegal is hiding property deeds. Shall I go on?"

Seething, she whipped open the folder and scrawled her name on the contract.

Hans slipped it from her fingers when she was finished and said, "Well done. My assistant will be in momentarily with the rest of the paperwork for you to sign. And don't worry, we'll file everything correctly. Hopefully it won't take you too long and you can take advantage of a sunny day in the city."

She glared at Turner. "So, you got what you wanted after all? Your fancy company to buy the properties for you. Look down your nose at me all you want, but you're going to do what any intelligent businessman would do and turn it in a huge development. Those people don't know the gem they have in Graciella." She huffed and turned away.

She was wrong on both accounts. He wasn't going to develop it the way she accused, and the people of Graciella knew exactly how rich they were. But he wasn't wasting a second explaining to her. He followed Hans to his office.

"Thank you," Turner said, his breath coming easily for the first time in days. "I could not have done that without you, financially or emotionally. I owe you one."

"Looks like you've got yourself some buildings to take care of," Hans said, clapping Turner on the back. He handed Turner the contract written to him, with a small investment by Klein Development. If Ms. Wells had looked closely, she would have seen that she'd just signed all three deeds over to Turner himself. They were right back where they belonged, almost.

"Now," Hans said, dismissing him, "go get your life back. I expect an invitation to the wedding. That's what you owe me, to grab onto your happiness, son."

Chapter Twenty-Eight

Lily was wrong. It was a hard thing to admit. Especially since Morenos were never wrong. Hardworking, caring, emotional, a little bit stubborn, but never wrong. Wouldn't it fit that the first time she acknowledged it, it was crushing?

Cleaning the theater was *not* the labor of love she'd imagined, she'd craved, she'd earned. Instead it was painful. Her entire life, solitude had been her pleasure. Loving people and being social was something she enjoyed, throwing herself into the fray of parties and friendships. But solitude, independence and autonomy were her foundation, where creativity thrived. All her solo successes looked different to her now that she was really all alone. Underneath, the current that threatened to finish her was the fear that Turner really wouldn't come back.

God, she'd been so, so stupid. He'd broken down so many of her walls and yet the one she'd never given to him, never really admitted to was that she wasn't good enough for him. Not that he'd never *see* her, but when he really did witness all her secret places, beyond the successful businesswoman, the curvy body, the vulnerable heart he seemed okay with, to the stubbornness, the temper, the rash idiot she was prone to be, he'd be disappointed. Like she thought he'd been all those years ago. Was she really just a silly, stupid, irrational little girl? A girl so easily left behind. A girl so easily forgotten.

Wiping the walls and the baseboards with the soft thick sponge back and forth, Lily found the monotony wasn't meditative or restorative or full of pleasure the way she'd imagined. Instead all the motion did was remind her, in her fierce need to be independent, to do and be everything to herself, that she'd shut out the one person in the world who was the perfect puzzle fit to her soul.

She'd completely overreacted, hadn't let him explain. Jesus, she'd *hit* him. But that wasn't even the worst part. She'd hurt him with her words. How could she ever have compared him and his brothers to T.D. Brockman? She knew deep in her heart that none of them were like that evil, emotionless man. But she'd let her stupid smashed gut overrule her sanity that night, thinking that Turner had played her mind, her body, her heart.

She'd been wrong too when she tried to tell Roxana and Miranda that she wasn't heartbroken. Good thing her friends were smart enough to see past her combination of super stupidity and denial and take care of her.

She'd considered going to Berlin, chasing after him, but the girls, Cruz and Adam had urged her to be patient and wait for him to return. Waiting was hard for her. Okay, she sucked at it. Add impatient — or was there a word for when a person had no patience at all, nopatient? — whatever the hell it was, she could add that to her list of qualities she wanted Turner to love. Her hand shook and she dropped the sponge. Flaws and all, she wanted Turner to love her. And the only thing she could do was wait.

Chapter Twenty-Nine

A moonless, clear night outside. Opening night and her theater sparkled too, just like the stars in the sky. It was finished. She'd dreamed about this day, what it would look like, and even during the rehab with the many moments of cursing, she'd always known it would turn out spectacular. There'd never been a doubt in her mind. However, she wasn't prepared for the empty feeling in her heart. Elated? Yes. Proud? Absolutely. Desolate had never factored into her endgame.

Standing in the back, looking down the rich midnight and gold carpeted aisles, it was infinitely prettier than her dreams. Accent shades of scarlet and gold glittered around her. The seats she'd had refurbished in Los Angeles were a deep red velvet with polished wood arms. Small lights lit a path down each aisle and above them glittered a gold ceiling with one large chandelier, so large she hadn't been able to hang it herself.

Behind her, the lobby stretched out with rich hardwood floors, an old concession stand full of popcorn, fun sodas for the kids and candy bags. She'd added a small wine bar in the corner where a waiter was handing out champagne. Smaller chandeliers anointed the ceiling and vintage movie posters graced the walls. At each of the three entrances to the movie seats, there was a bench, also covered in red velvet. People hummed around her, marveling over how beautiful everything looked.

The theater her father built had been fun. Her remake was glamorous, showy, enchanting. The way she'd dreamed it.

A grand celebration she'd been planning for months. Her greatest accomplishment so far. Maybe not the biggest, but the one closest to her heart.

She should be laughing, accepting hugs and compliments, basking in the glow. But because her heart had left her body, she felt outside of it all, hollow, not fully able to appreciate her hard work. Even the vintage donut machine she'd found and installed didn't make her smile. All she could think of with the aroma of fried dough dipped in sugar lingering around her was Turner.

All her work and accomplishments meant nothing without him. There was a teeny part of her that thought he did love her, that he would come back even with the lure of his fabulous job in Berlin, the thrill of the next big project, all the money he could dream about. That if she could simply be patient and wait for him, he'd return to her.

But he hadn't. Wow, her heart hurt.

And adding to her already bruised heart was the fact that her father hadn't woken in three days. Every stage of this shitty disease was worse than the one before. And each one surprised her with that bombshell. Like tripping on each new land mine of pain and grief. One more stage to witness, to mourn before he could finally be set free from what Lily thought of now as his prison. When she hadn't been cleaning the theater, she'd been at his bedside. Every one of her employees had stepped up to help where they could.

"You look miserable," Roxanna whispered in her ear.

Lily didn't even have the energy to argue. Miserable was being kind. Not that her outfit wasn't killer. Miranda had made her a stunning dress, sleeveless, one-shoulder, fitted and ruched on top, that draped from black into red and hit below her knees. She wore mile-high strappy heels with a rhinestone closure. One large, glittery barrette held her curls back to the side, leaving the rest to dance around her face. But without her heart, she hardly cared. Apparently, she wasn't able to hide it. She'd thought going through with the opening would be a good thing.

She'd been wrong.

"You know he's been gone less than a week, honey. He'll be back."

"How can you be so sure?" Lily could barely get the words out. She was done with her bravado when it came to Turner. *Someone please tell me how it will all turn out.* Her world was flat and she didn't know what to do about that. And the way her heart ached, less than a week felt like decades.

"Because I know everything and I'm always right." Roxanna kissed her cheek. Lily nearly rolled her eyes then, but Rox *was* always right. "You designed a thing of beauty, honey. Your parents would be so proud of you. I'm proud of you."

"You going to give us a show or what, Ms. Moreno?"

"Who the hell are you and what have you done with my friend?" Lily asked Adam who gave her a quick bow. He was all dolled up in a navy suit, with cowboy boots and a hat. "I don't recognize you. You should clean up more often." It was good that he looked nothing like Turner with his red hair and blue eyes and constant grin. After she'd lashed out at all three of them, Cruz and Adam had both tried to assure her everything would be okay, that it wasn't what she assumed. She'd tried to listen, she really had, but the constant ringing in her ears made most of what they said a muddled mess. At any rate, once she'd recovered and realized what a crazy person she'd acted like, she'd been grateful they'd forgiven her.

"Looking stunning, darlin'." Adam gave her a gentle hug. He'd always been like that, gentle for such a large man. Cruz and Miranda had already greeted her and found seats right up front. Everyone else followed when the lights flickered. It was bittersweet watching people stream down the aisles to their seats. And all of them ridiculously happy. She wanted to turn and run. But she'd done plenty of that in the last few weeks. And this was supposed to be her triumph. Roxanna insisted she had to stay and take in the joy and wonder from her friends and family. Ready or not, she had a speech to give.

From her view on stage looking out at the full theater, everyone sparkled in dressy clothes. They ate popcorn and chocolate, sugary donut holes. An excited wave of conversation rolled through the seats, everyone guessing what the very first movie would be.

Lily was glad she hadn't run. This was her gem, and nothing could mar it. Later, she'd bury her wounds in leftover donuts and sleep for a week.

"Good evening," she began, and the crown broke into applause before she could continue. Tears filled her eyes. These were her people. This was her place, and no matter how much she hurt right now, Rox had been right — Lily needed this.

Taking a deep breath, she brushed away the tear that had escaped and continued, "I'm so excited for you all to be here. And I'm grateful for each and every one of you for supporting me. I love this town and I love all of you." She'd meant to say more, but tears choked her voice. They all knew how she felt about them, about the community. "It's showtime," she finished on a whisper.

She put the microphone back in its stand and was about to carry it off stage when movement from the side caught her eye. Handsome, sexy, beaming movement in the form of Turner Brockman striding onstage, dressed in a dark gray suit with a black shirt, carrying an envelope and an enormous bouquet of red and black calla lilies. Lily froze.

"What?" Her heart nearly stopped. Then it jumped in her chest, a new start. Her heart was beating again. He was here, her Turner. Finally home.

Handing her the bouquet, he said quietly, "May I?" And he took the mic from her hands.

"I hope you'll all bear with me a moment," he said, facing the crowd. "I need to make a quick apology to our Lily." And he didn't wait for their acknowledgment.

"What's going on?" Lily glanced around. The entire audience froze like her. Or maybe not. They all had huge smiles on their faces.

He stepped closer, gently took her hand and spoke. The warmth of his hand holding hers nearly brought her to her knees. "Lily Moreno. I haven't felt home in a long time. Even as a kid when I lived here, I was always on guard or trying to prove myself. Afraid. Confused. Powerless. I thought it would be the same when I came back. I thought I would bury a few ghosts, get the hell out and be done. But you righted my entire world. Well, first you flipped it upside down a few times." Adam's laugh boomed out over the audience. "Suddenly everything made sense. My home is with you. And whether or not you'll have me, I have this for you." He took the flowers from her and placed the envelope in her hands.

She felt the weight of it, the soft paper, but couldn't look away from his eyes. Eyes that said, *I love you. I need you. I'm hoping you'll love me back.*

"What?" was all she could get out.

"Open it!" someone shouted from the audience.

Her hands shook and she nearly dropped the envelope. But she managed to find the opening and remove a thick bunch of folded papers.

"I don't understand," she said. "What is all of this?" Tears blurred her vision. "Damn tears." She wiped them away and was trying to read the words when she felt Turner wrap his arms around her to steady her. She breathed him in and let his touch heal her. "You're really here?" she whispered into his chest.

He nodded. "I bought you something."

"A ring!" Miranda's and Roxanna's voices squealed together and Lily heard the gentle roll of laughter before the quiet descended again.

"I thought you'd like this more than a ring. The other side of the block. The three properties T.D.

bought and sold out from under us. They belong to you now."

Lily filtered through the documents. Through her tears, she found the hardware store.

"I tried to explain that night in the kitchen, but I wasn't certain everything would go my way. Hans offered to help me get them back. I had to go to Berlin and face Elizabeth Wells. We needed her to think Klein Development was making her an offer and I didn't want to get your hopes up if I ruined the deal in the end. I knew it was the most important deal of my life. Surprise!"

Ooos and aaahhs murmured through the rows full of people, her family and friends.

"I signed them all over to you. I know you'll take good care of them or see them back where they belong. If you'll let me, I'd like to help you, work with you, be your partner. I'd also like to be yours, if you'll let me back into your heart. I love you, Liliana Moreno, and I want to take on the world with you."

She leaned in and did what she'd been wanting to do since he came on stage, wrapped her arms around him and kissed him as if it were the last great kiss she'd ever have. Or the first of many, many more.

Turner lifted her up and spun her around and the entire audience stood, cheering and clapping for them.

"You got a standing ovation," Turner said.

"No, *we* did, my love. I love you so much, Turner. I've loved you since I was just a silly girl with a crush. I am so, so sorry for my behavior. I went off the deep end and yelled rotten things. Please forgive me. I can't be without you. I need you and I love you with all my heart."

"Nothing to forgive, my siren. I love your passion."

She squeezed him tight and, with happy tears streaming down her cheeks, added, "One question, though. Can I have a ring too?"

He laughed into her neck and her entire world soared. "Are you saying you want to be my wife, lovely Lily?"

"No, Turner. I want to be your everything. Like you are my everything."

"I guess we should see if this fit, then." He set her down, slipped a ring from his pocket and placed it on her finger.

"Turner," she whispered. "It's the prettiest thing I've ever seen. It's a ruby."

He tilted her chin up. "A ruby suits you. But it's not the prettiest thing." He placed his lips on hers gently. "You are," he whispered. And this time she kissed him while her beautiful community cheered and whistled around them.

Epilogue

Normally Lily couldn't think of a more beautiful time on the farm than late spring, when everything rioted into bloom. The apple blossoms perfumed the air. Tulips, poppies and roses opened and brightened the gardens. Sugar snap peas climbed up their vines and strawberries went crazy. Rows of salad greens lined up like soldiers between the troughs of dirt as they rolled over the land. Everything coming alive.

But, wow, this late summer day in August was absolutely brilliant. Not only from the gazillions of colorful dahlias and towering yellow and red sunflowers, the cabbage plants and tomatoes ready for harvesting, or the apple tree branches heavy with fruit. Or the gorgeous new north wing, so close to being finished. *But from love.*

Lily bet Miranda would have happily gotten married in the new wing, where the café would be, if it hadn't been for the land. Miranda had fallen in love with Brockman Farms as much as she'd fallen for Cruz. And the outdoor ceremony was the loveliest Lily had ever seen. They'd gotten married in the grass right next to the fifty or so rose bushes that had been a part of Brockman Farms before even the main house had been built. Lily loved the image, the history here, and now the bright new potential. A perfect marriage.

They'd eaten at the long tables gorgeously set with linens and vases of farm flowers, the meal catered by Miguel and Roxanna's Mexican restaurant. Now they were dancing off all that delicious food and drink under a tent lit with gazillions of tiny white fairy lights.

Lily grabbed another mini cupcake from the dessert table — she'd already tasted one vanilla and devoured two sopapillas — but one couldn't let a cupcake go to waste. She watched the center of the dance floor. Miranda in her long, sleeveless red dress stole the show with Cruz's arms wrapped around her as he dipped her in a long low arch, nose to nose sharing intimate secrets. Turner and Adam danced with Miguel and Roxanna's girls in one big circle, all four of them. Adam held hands with two and Turner held Ana's hand with one of his and close to his chest he cradled a sleeping Serafina, the poor baby tuckered out from the long, fun day. Although the munchkin looked pretty content to sleep against Turner. Who wouldn't be? Beside them, snuggled together, were Miguel and Roxanna lost in their own slow dance zone, even though the song playing around them was a lively old band number. Lily would snuggle and slow dance too if she were Roxanna who hardly ever got a break from being a super mom to her six kiddos.

I wonder what kind of mom I'll be. She smiled at the thought of Turner as a dad. The month since he'd come back had been a roller coaster of emotions, some involving just that topic, motherhood. At first, Lily had been grateful she hadn't, as Roxanna hinted, been pregnant. Her sickness that day had been heartsick from thinking Turner had betrayed her.

Then, two days after their engagement night at the theater, her papá had passed away. Quietly, in his sleep, almost as if he knew Lily wouldn't be left alone. She and Turner were present, and it was both the hardest moment of her life and the most precious to witness him finally at peace. When she'd breathed deep with the knowledge of her father's death, and let the tears come, she'd mourned not only the loss of him, but so many losses to come. Like the gut punch that if she ever did get to be a mom, her children would never know her father or her mother. Watching Turner dance with those little girls was both lovely and saddening. The grief hit her again. She knew it would never fully go away. It helped to know she was surrounded by love and that she didn't have to handle all her grief alone.

The song ended, Turner handed the baby off to Adam and headed directly for her with that sexy smile on his face, the one full of secrets. Oh, Lord, what was he up to now? She'd had champagne, but it was all his hotness that made her swoon.

"Hi," she said, nearly breathless when he stopped right in front of her. Turner Brockman in a tux, smiling at her, was the most beautiful thing she'd ever seen. It sure was delicious fun to be able to act like a giddy schoolgirl over him and not give one hoot what anyone thought.

"Gorgeous," he said. His eyes moved a fraction away from hers to her lips and he reached out with his thumb to wipe something from the edge of her mouth. "Chocolate?"

"Do you want kids?" she blurted. And his eyes shot back up to meet hers. His smile changed to her favorite, that soft one he saved for her alone. A smile full of love and vulnerability, as though he couldn't believe his luck. His own way of swooning over her. Then he moved in and tucked his warm hands around her to pull her flush against him. "I think I want to be a mom." Whispered, reverent words she could barely get past the emotions filling her.

"You, Liliana Moreno, would be an awesome mom," Turner whispered back.

"I think the same about you, that you'll be such a great dad, Turner."

"Mmm." He kissed her neck and moved them toward the dance floor where Etta James now mesmerized them all with her deep, raw vocals. "Good thing we're getting hitched." He twirled her into him and swayed with her held tight under the glittering lights, love and family all around them. "Know what else I love about this topic?" he asked.

"What?" She could read his mind. "How much fun we'll have trying to get pregnant?"

"Exactly." He winked at her and Lily stood on her tiptoes and kissed her first love, her forever love.

"Ready to go?" she teased. "We could start right now."

"As soon as this song is over. Having you in my arms while we dance is a moment I want to savor, just like I plan on savoring every moment with you."

Want to see more from this author? Here's a taster for you to enjoy!

Rescue Me: Salvaging Love
Sara Ohlin

Excerpt

Ellie was a soggy, soapy mess of bubbles and puppy fur. By some miracle, a few strands of her hair had survived the battle to bathe Chewie, one of the litter of four she'd found at the front door of her clinic, dirty, scrawny and huddled together in a cardboard box.

It wasn't the first time since she'd opened her vet clinic four years ago that animals had been abandoned at the door. Once, she'd even found a lovebird waiting for her. One lovebird. Everyone knew lovebirds were a pair. Ellie couldn't stand to see animals abandoned or put down, not if there was the slimmest chance someone could love them and give them a home.

Fortunately, these four babies would be adopted soon. Puppies always were. They were part Lab and part a whole bunch of mutt. Chewie was chocolate brown, like his namesake, and his hair was velvety and curly, more retriever-like. His shimmery brown baby eyes filled with longing every time he gazed at her. *I might have to keep this one.* As she poured water over him, he launched himself into her arms trying to cling to the large rubber apron she wore. Before she could disentangle him and put his butt back in the water, the bell over the front door rang. *Damn!* She'd meant to lock it. She kept Chewie attached to her chest with one hand, grabbed a towel to wrap around him with her other and headed out front.

Holy cow! "Can I…ah, help you?" The man stood by the front window, silhouetted by the fading evening light. Huge and gorgeous with rugged tan skin, black hair curling over his collar and the coolest blue-green eyes she'd ever seen. Ellie almost sighed, but that flash of beauty disappeared in an instant. Anger radiated from him.

"What the hell is going on, Ken?" he said into his phone, but he pierced her with his gaze.

His anger vibrated over them. Chewie started shaking in her arms and buried his head in the towel. "I'm sorry, sir, but can I help you? This is my —"

"What do I mean?" he ignored her to yell into his phone. "I'm standing here on my property that still has tenants in it. Explain!"

Sheesh. She leaned back with the force of his words. "It's okay, baby," she cooed to the shivering puppy in her arms. "Sir," she called louder this time, "we're closed right now and you're scaring the animals. If you wouldn't mind taking your phone call outside, I —"

He sliced his hand up to silence her.

Excuse me? She was not about to let this foul-mouthed jerk boss her around, but before she could say anything else, he hung up. "If you were closed, why was your door unlocked?"

"What?" It wasn't merely his size or harsh tone that had her brain malfunctioning. She couldn't keep up with his line of questioning.

"Your door," he said, his tone singeing her. "Why would a woman like you leave her door unlocked while she's here by herself?"

'*A woman like you?*' Ellie flinched. She didn't even want to know what he meant by that comment. She'd spent eighteen years of her life with people putting her down. No way in hell she was going to listen to more of it, not after she'd clawed her way out of that filth so long ago. She chose to focus on only part of what he said.

"I'm not alone." She scrubbed the soft puppy.

"Jesus." He closed his eyes.

She certainly didn't know what *that* meant. His swearing said a lot, but at the same time it didn't really say anything.

"Would you mind not swearing?"

"Excuse me?"

"I said, would you —"

"I heard you."

Okay, now she was getting angry. "Listen. I don't know who you are or what you're doing here, but, like I said, we're closed for the evening and I need to get home. You can make an appointment or come back in the morning when we open." God, she hoped he didn't come back.

"You should have been closed for good a week ago. Closed and vacated."

"What? What do you mean? This is my clinic. I signed a lease through the end of the year. That's seven months away."

"I know when the end of the year is."

The man had a degree in condescending behavior. His tone, his attitude, his entire demeanor said power and money, and the tailored gray suit, black dress shirt and shoes all bragged of wealth. The way he tried to silence her with his hand in the air. She couldn't stand people thinking they were better than everyone else. It got her hackles up. That and the way he studied her, assessing.

"I was stating the terms so you could realize your mistake and apologize for barging in here with your atrocious behavior and yelling at me."

He stared at her again. His features transformed from a pissed-off beast to a quiet, controlled predator. As if he carefully leashed his temper, and instead saw her as a problem to be solved. His eyes were calculating. It sent a nervous tingle up her spine.

"Well?" she prompted, trying to act braver than she felt. Chewie's heartbeat raced against hers. He wiggled to get loose from her tight hold.

"Terms have changed." He raised an eyebrow. Those eyes of his were a mysterious blue-green, like a deep pristine lake surrounded by mountains. And when he wasn't yelling, his voice soothed. He took a step toward her which jarred her out of her observations. She leaned back.

"What terms? Who are you?" She had to look up now. Jesus, he was well over six feet tall.

"Jackson Kincaid. I'm the new owner of this block. I'm tearing the entire thing down. Everyone was supposed to be vacated last week at the latest," he finished, delivering the blow to her gut just when the wriggling mass in her arms threw himself onto the floor and shook his sudsy, wet puppy body all over the man. Unable to find traction on the slippery floor, the pup flopped over on his back and clung to Jackson's pants with his tiny claws.

"Christ!" He reached down and plucked the pup up into the air, holding him away from his body.

"The new owner? Of the whole block? And you're tearing it all down?" She was surprised she could even find her voice at the shock. "You can't."

"I can," he said, glaring at her with that raised-eyebrow thing he did that made her feel ten instead of twenty-seven.

"Can't." She'd found her voice again, getting pissed.

"Can," he said, leaning in.

"You're a bully!" Anger heated her blood. "You don't even know me or the Heelys, or Carl and his daughter. I know your kind. And I won't let you come in here and intimidate me."

"You won't?" He looked at her questioningly. Or was he teasing her? She'd been so busy yelling, it almost sounded now as if he were fighting back laughter.

"No, I won't."

"And how do you plan to stop me?"

But she didn't get a chance to speak because Chewie let loose and peed all over Mr. Bully, drenching his perfect-fitting suit and his expensive leather dress shoes.

Ellie watched, frozen in place while he blinked. *Oh, shit!* "I…I am so sorry. He's just a, well—"

"Puppy. Got it," he clipped.

"Someone left a litter at the door and I had to get them clean. He's not trained."

"Yeah. I got that too."

"Here," she said quietly, trading him a towel for Chewie.

"Fuck! This day keeps getting better. Slime of the earth in my office earlier. Get over here to check out my buildings, find the tenants still here, an ignorant blonde and now I have puppy piss all over me." He wiped at his wet shirt and jacket with the towel.

She soothed Chewie and bristled at the *ignorant blonde* comment.

"Look, I'm sorry about what happened, but there's no need to be rude. You don't know me, which means you don't get to call me ignorant. What *I* know from *your* behavior is that you're an arrogant jerk who needs lessons in manners."

His eyes met hers, and the heat in them made her suck in her breath. Okay, maybe she'd gotten carried away and should *really* learn when to stay quiet. He acted like a jerk, but it wasn't like she had to point it out to him. Belatedly she realized it was kind of like teasing a hungry lion.

"Not ignorant?" His voice had turned low. Yup, definitely poking a lion. "You're here alone. It's dark. Every store along this street is closed. It's a sketchy neighborhood at best, and you leave your door unlocked?"

"Why do you care?" Ellie was confused by this entire conversation.

"Why?" He prowled closer. Okay, she should definitely be more careful about locking her door. "You. Here. Alone. Any cracked-up junkie could come right in and take what he wanted." He waved his hand up and down her body to indicate what that might mean.

"Now you're freaking me out *and* being rude." Her voice wasn't above a whisper, but he heard it.

"Good!"

"Good?"

"Yeah, maybe you'll be freaked out enough next time to lock your fucking door."

Okay, she was exhausted, and hurt by his words, although she didn't understand why, since he was nothing to her. She wasn't good in situations like this — no matter how many years and miles away she was from her childhood, nasty people still affected her ability to be strong. It was painful to realize she hadn't gotten better at handling it at all. "Right. I understand," she began without any of the anger or passion lacing her words. "And I, ah, appreciate your concern, even if it's delivered in a yelling, jerky way, but you don't need to worry about me."

He braced back as if she'd slapped him. "You're kidding me?"

"No. Anyway, my night vet tech should be here any minute. Plus, I have Buffy. She's a great judge of character."

"Buffy?"

Ellie pointed toward the corner where her ten-year-old, one-hundred-pound Rottweiler slept on her dog bed, snoring away.

"Right, I can see how Buffy, who hasn't moved a muscle except to snore since I got here, is a perfect guard dog."

Ellie brushed back the curls that had slipped out of her ponytail. "If we continue this conversation tonight, you're going to throw your stuck-up disbelief and insults in my face, and as pleasant as it seems to be for you, it's not for me.

"I've been here since six, on my feet all day, which normally I don't mind because I love my job, but I had a horrible surgery on a dog. My assistant left at noon. I still have to get this little guy and his siblings settled for the night, which means fed, taken out to pee, shots and crates. I haven't eaten since breakfast. Dinner is a peanut butter and jelly sandwich before I face-plant into bed. You come in and threaten my clinic, no correction, my *dream*, which I worked my butt off to open. Maybe you could come back tomorrow, or we could meet for coffee and you can tell me, if you really are the new owner, what I have to do to convince you not to tear this block of buildings down. Then we can both go our separate ways and never see each other again."

It almost hurt her to say those words, because even though he was a total jerk, he was beautiful to look at. But horrors could hide behind beautiful appearances, something she was all too aware of. After all, her mother was a gorgeous model, but underneath she was crazy mean, and Ellie was the one who had taken the brunt of it.

He studied her while she spoke, silent and assessing again. Then he reached by her to grab one of her business cards from the counter. "Dr. Ellie Blevins, you think you can convince me not to tear this bag of bones down and build up a new condo development that will make billions?"

Billions? Did every battle she fought in this life have to be so outrageously difficult? This block was special. It wasn't only her clinic. It was the bakery, the hardware store that Carl and his daughter ran, her friend Ruby's spa, Lachlan's pub. This neighborhood burst with potential. And the park at the end of the block right along the river was lovely. The bonds she'd formed here, the true friendships, would make her fight back, even if she didn't feel brave enough for herself.

"It's not a bag of bones. It's a block of old, historic buildings that need love and care," she began. But standing there, taking in his polished rich-man strength, it was futile to convince him of anything. "You know what? Deal me the death blow now. I'd like to review the lease I signed before I throw in the towel and start looking for a new space and a new home, because I can tell there's no way you and I will ever be on the same page."

"New home?"

"What?" she said.

"You said, 'a new space and a new home'?"

"I live in the apartment above the French Connection Bakery. Mr. and Mrs. Heely have owned it for twenty-five years." There she was, exhausted-sharing again. And there he stood intense-staring. She closed her eyes at the craziest, weirdest conversation she'd ever had, and realized Chewie was asleep on her chest with his tiny head nuzzled in her neck. *Oh, soft love*, she thought, *if only people were more like dogs, so trusting, kind, and loving.*

"One month," he said.

"One month to be out of — "

"I'll give you one month to try to convince me."

"I… What?"

"You spend time with me for the next month. We get to know each other, and you can state your case."

"Spend time with you?" *Is he insane?*

"You said you wanted to try to convince me to change my mind."

"Oh," she whispered, confused again.

"You open tomorrow?"

"Yes," she said quickly, thinking maybe they'd tested each other's patience enough for one evening.

"Right, then. Tomorrow. Lock your door." Then he was gone, leaving her more confused than ever.

"Lock your door!" he yelled from outside, startling her out of her spot.

She went to the door, locked it, drew the blinds down and blew out a breath. "What in the heck just happened? I feel like a tornado blew through here and tossed us sideways into outer space. And what does 'tomorrow' mean? Is he coming back? Am I supposed to appear before him like a magician?"

She looked at Chewie and spoke into the empty waiting area with Buffy chasing squirrels in her dreams. *Holy cow! Holy freaking cow! This place is everything to me, more than my hopes and dreams – it's my safe place.* One single month to convince an angry lion not to eat her up? She might be an awesome veterinarian, but there were absolutely no instructions for how to communicate with a beast like Jackson Kincaid.

Home of Erotic Romance

Sign up for our newsletter and find out about all our romance book releases, eBook sales and promotions, sneak peeks and FREE romance books!

About the Author

Sara Ohlin has lived all over the United States, but her heart keeps getting pulled back to the Pacific Northwest where it belongs. For years she has been writing creative non-fiction and memoir and feels that writing helps her make sense of this crazy world. She devours books and can often be found shushing her two hilarious kids so that she can finish reading. When she isn't reading or writing, she'll most likely be in the kitchen cooking up something scrumptious, a French macaron, shrimp scampi, a fun date-night-in dinner with her sexy husband, or perhaps her next love story.

Sara loves to hear from readers. You can find her contact information, website details and author profile page at https://www.totallybound.com